"For the next month, you actually have a few more chances to run into me," she said.

"Oh yeah, what happens next month?"

"I go back to school and mold the minds of Chicago's youth."

"Well then, I guess I have to take a lot more time off before children steal you away."

They approached the door of his neighbor's apartment. His own was two doors away but he made no move to continue on. Before he got a chance to ask for her number, Maddie put the key into the lock. "I guess you will. I look forward to it." She slipped through the now open door, and closed it, leaving him standing there.

He blew out a breath and scratched the back of his head, starting toward the door to his own condo. The sound of Mrs. Marlow's doorknob turning made him stop and look back as Maddie popped her head out. "Monday, Wednesday, Friday from one thirty to two."

She flashed him a dazzling smile that sent a jolt through his body and hurriedly shut the door again. He smiled and walked back to the door, a new energy in his step.

For once, he was looking forward to a Monday.

The Robbery Across the Hall

by

Emilie Barage

Murder for Your Thoughts, Book 2

The Robbery Across the Hall

Cover Art by *Kim Mendoza*

The Wild Rose Press, Inc.
PO Box 708
Adams Basin, NY 14410-0708
Visit us at www.thewildrosepress.com

Publishing History
First Edition, 2023
Trade Paperback ISBN 978-1-5092-4912-1
Digital ISBN 978-1-5092-4913-8

Murder for Your Thoughts, Book 2
Published in the United States of America

Dedication

To my Mom and Dad, thanks for everything but especially for never hanging up the phone when I call you crying about stress.
To my wonderful friends who bring me such laughter and love, I couldn't have done this without you.
To TikTok, who was there when I needed to zone out.

Chapter One

The scent of Lake Michigan, mixed with the aromas of my sunscreen and a bag of dog poop, creates an offending smell. I toss the baggie into a nearby trash can and look down at Rascal, a golden-doodle mix, who sits staring at me and wagging his tail.

"Nope. No treats until we're back in your house buddy."

As if he understands me, Rascal begins to pull at his leash, heading in the direction of his Gold Coast apartment.

I rein him in, causing him to slow to a normal pace while we walk back. I find myself wishing I was able to control my students as easily as the dogs I walk during the summer. Most of the year I teach fifth grade at a Chicago public school where I'm only known as Ms. Conor. I have always loved teaching and I grow pretty attached to a different batch of kids every year but there is always that handful that need a bit more attention. By the end of spring semester, I'm always ready for the summer vacation.

Right out of college and my first year of teaching, summer vacation came and went—and with it, all my money. At twenty-four, I didn't realize that budgeting was a necessity. Now, as a twenty-nine-year-old veteran, I knew how to better handle money: by getting a summer job that pays more.

When looking for the ideal gig, I knew I wanted something that allowed me to make my own hours. I would be earning money but still have the ability to go to the beach if I felt the urge. I have been walking dogs for five years now and love it, especially since I have such sweet repeat clients like Rascal.

Exiting the underpass that connects the neighborhood to the lakefront, I walk down Division, toward State Street. When I first started with Ruffin' It, the dog-walking service, I took jobs closer to home in Wicker Park. Then I quickly realized that taking walks in the more affluent neighborhoods meant bigger tips. I now exclusively take jobs in this neighborhood. While I've never lived here, nor could ever afford to, I pretty much know it like the back of my hand. After turning south on State Street, Rascal and I walk the familiar route down toward the Newberry Library and the rows of townhouses surrounding Washington Square Park.

Rascal is my last walk of the day. I tried to hit up the high rises along Lakeshore Drive first and worked my way back toward the townhomes, getting me closer toward the bus and therefore shortening my trip home. Walking up the elaborate stone steps, I open the door of an ash gray home with a large oak entryway. Rascal is rewarded with his treat; I give him some love and attention for a few minutes and then start on my way home.

Popping in my earbuds, I walk the few blocks to the bus stop. The newest episode of the *Murder for Your Thoughts* podcast has just been posted. Originally a blog, it became so popular, the creator, a woman only known as RJ, decided to turn it into a bi-weekly podcast. Now, I am addicted. I still go back and read the blog every once in a while, but the podcast is so convenient, I'm able to listen while I walk. As I wait for the latest episode to load, I mentally go over my schedule for the next few days.

Tomorrow, Friday, I'm only scheduled for two walks, both in a swanky high rise. Before I do that, I need to go into Ruffin' It to pick up a paycheck. I'm not looking forward to it because it means crossing paths with Matt Simon my ex. Once that difficult but necessary chore is completed, I'll be free to use the weekend to sit and relax all day and drink with my roommates before they go out with their respective partners at night.

Lost in thought, I jump as the podcast starts playing, shocking me back into reality. The bus pulls up and I settle in for the ride, letting RJ's soft voice fill my ears.

"What's up Murder Heads? RJ here, back for another episode of Murder for Your Thoughts. If you've been listening to recent episodes, you'll know that I'm taking a bit of a different approach this month. I figured I'd take a stab at crimes in general, murder, rape, larceny, and similarities behind them, then talk about famous stories linked to the topic.

"Last week we talked about Murders of Passion; the most popular reason for murders and the types of people who commit them. Then I told you all about the Ballad of Annie Philer, also known as the New York Nanny. She was the one who targeted her boss's wife. I also gave you a newer one about Erin McIver, the salesgirl who said she was only defending herself against her ex-boyfriend after he tried to kill her. One old story, one contemporary.

"This week I'm covering home robberies. Why specifically home robberies, you might ask? Well, I will

tell you.

"I was originally going to do a week on robberies in general, but I was sent a very interesting article from a very famous murder head *cough Holly Harrison cough* about a string of robberies that have been making their way through Chicago. I figured I'd kill two birds with one stone and tell you all a story and give Chicago Murder Heads a heads up to look out.

"This one, I'll admit, was a difficult topic to research. It's not like killers, where you can check things off a list like they suffered a previous head injury, or they wet the bed till they were well into puberty or have a history of animal abuse. Robberies are different. People can be driven to them by desperation, greed, or blackmail. Thieves can research the targets, studying when they'll be out of the house, what objects they desire to steal, or they can be seized by a moment of opportunity and take it.

"The Glitter Gang, for example, was a group of teenagers famous for monitoring celebrities by checking their social media posts to see when they would be out of the house, or filming on location. They would break in, take the designer-labeled clothing, jewelry and shoes..."

While RJ speaks on each member of the Glitter Gang, I look out the window of the bus, watching as we drive underneath the highway that separates individual neighborhoods. The updated townhomes soon dwindle and become replaced by storefronts and bars. The bus goes deeper into Wicker Park, and I watch hordes of twenty-somethings enjoying the summer weather, dining and drinking on patios with music blaring.

I hop off at my stop and realize I have accidentally tuned out to the voice in my ears. Refocusing on the words, I make my way down the residential street toward home.

"...I mean, once you get a movie based on your actions, you've peaked. Anyway, what is happening in Chicago right now? Well, funnily enough, the Chicago robberies actually started farther down the coast in Indiana and have worked their way up north. The latest robbery was in the Loop. If I were a betting woman, I would say the Gold Coast is next. Keep your eyes peeled for creeps scoping out all the old ladies who like to deck themselves out in their jewels."

The scents from multiple backyard barbeques fill my nose as I take the steps to my third-story walk-up. Shifting between the five different keys to find the correct one for the front door, I notice movement out of the corner of my eye. Looking up, I saw my neighbors, Kelly and Ryan Maller, walking out the door with their two young daughters.

"Look, girls, it's Maddie," Kelly says to her daughters.

The girls, Amy and Ally are wearing matching green sundresses, their blonde hair pulled into low pigtails. Ally, the younger of the two, pulls her thumb out of her mouth and waves enthusiastically, mimicking her older sister.

I smile and wave back. "Hi, girls. Maybe I'll see you sometime this weekend?"

Their cheers of excitement flood me with warmth as I make my way up the three flights of stairs. I love that I know my neighbors. In all the different locations I've lived in while being a resident of Chicago, this area was by far the most comforting and familiar. My mood only gets better when I open the door and my eyes land on the scene in front of me.

Sarah and Stephanie, it seemed, have purchased the entirety of the grocery store's cheese section and laid it out on the dining room table along with three bottles of wine. Sarah's long bright-red hair falls into her face as she pours the contents of one of the bottles into three separate glasses.

She looks up as I walk in the door. "Perfect timing! This one is for you!"

Laughing, I ask, "What's the occasion?"

Sarah pretends to be offended, flipping the hair back from her face, allowing me to see her fair skin and brown eyes full of mischief. "Um it's Thursday. That is the occasion."

From the kitchen in the back of the apartment my other roommate, Stephanie, chimes in with, "Yeah. Thursday. Get with it, Maddie."

I fling my bag to the floor and run into my room while yelling, "Let me put on comfier clothes."

While digging through my drawers for cotton shorts, my thoughts drift to my roommates. Sarah, a computer programmer, had been a friend since we met each other at a birthday party. When I officially got a job and made the move to Chicago, I initially rented a one-bedroom apartment. Realizing that a fifth-grade teacher could not afford to live on her own, I began to cast my net, looking for a roommate. It just so happened that Sarah was also looking for a roommate. After we found this apartment, we put out an ad looking for a third roommate and Stephanie thankfully answered.

Steph is a kind, compassionate person who works in human resources and provided a perfect balance to Sarah's sharp wit and my sarcasm. The first weekend we all lived together, she took it upon herself to cook us a three-course dinner complete with homemade dinner rolls and fancy cocktails. Sarah and I decided then and there that she could never leave us until she got married. Luckily, Steph has stayed.

Though we could not come from more different backgrounds, the three of us live well together. Sarah has classic Irish looks with shocking red hair and fair skin. Stephanie is all blonde hair and blue eyes, looking every bit the innocent cartoon princess that she is in real life and I'm the naturally tanned skinned and caramel colored hair gal who rounds out our living color wheel. We hang out, binge on TV shows, go out for drinks. I easily call them my closest friends. They've been there for me, especially after the breakup with Matt.

"Give me wine please," I say as I come out of my room.

Sarah hands me the full glass of the chilled liquid while Stephanie stands over the table shoveling cheese into her mouth. "So, what are we doing this weekend?"

Sarah takes a long swig, "Mark is coming over".

Stephanie swallows the cheese, "So is Jeff. Let's hit up some bars? Maybe go to the park?"

"Fifth wheeling?" I ask. "Yeah, I'm up for that."

Stephanie big blue eyes fill with concern. "You know we can easily round up Jeff and Mark's single friends if you're ready to meet someone. We've been waiting for you to give the okay."

Shaking my head, I swallow another mouthful of wine. "I was just teasing. I love going out with you guys. While I appreciate the offer of pimping out your boyfriend's friends, I am okay with being single for the moment."

Sarah grabs the bottle, and while walking out to our balcony calls out over her shoulder, "Steph, didn't you know? Maddie wants fate to bring her the next beau."

We follow her outside and sit in the padded chairs that overlook the backyard. "I just want to meet someone organically, that's all."

Stephanie smiles. "I think that's kind of nice. You do you, and if you get tired of the organic route, you let me know."

Sarah chimes in, "I think it's fine, too. We don't want another Matt now."

We all clink glasses, and in that moment I feel content for things to stay the same for the time being.

Chapter Two

"I think you're going to fit in just fine here, Jack."

Smiling and nodding for what felt like the tenth time that hour, Jack Delgado felt his cheeks start to hurt. Expressions of excitement became more and more fake with each new person he met. At the beginning of the week, he started working at The People's Law Collective, a private criminal defense firm. Now, being Friday, he finally crossed off "meet everyone" from his To Do List. He was exhausted.

Given where he'd come from, he knew it was important to make a good first impression if he wanted to jump seamlessly into the work. He'd wanted to work in the low-income defense office since early in law school. He'd wanted to help people and use a law degree for good. He also knew that his dream job was not going to make him a ton of money, but he had lots of debt to pay off. The solution came after he secured an internship at a private firm, then got hired on after graduation. After a few years of late nights and working extra weekends, he managed to be debt free, build up a nice nest egg and buy a new apartment. Then, with great recommendations and an impressive resume, it was not difficult to snag a position at his dream job: working for the People's Law Collective.

Sandra, his immediate supervisor, gave him a sympathetic smile. "I know starting a new job is a lot to take on, but you've seemed to adjust quite well this week. I know you must be a bit tired."

Jack's fake smile was replaced with a real grin. "Meeting and remembering everyone I've interacted with this week can be a bit tiring, but I just can't wait to get started." He couldn't help but look past Sandra's shoulder into his new office at all the boxes that still needed to be unpacked.

She followed the line of sight and gave him a knowing smile. "Why don't you finish settling in and then head out? Summer hours are in place, so you probably won't get any cases assigned till Monday."

With a brisk nod of thanks, he walked into his new space to finish unpacking. The only thing that was left to do really was unload the box of desk supplies. He had lucked out when he was assigned a bigger office than most newer hires would have gotten. The small bookshelf was filled with the reference books he had collected over the years. The black leather loveseat nestled in a corner with a floor lamp at its side, the coffee table held a set of stone, Cubs-themed coasters. He'd done a good job this week. As soon as he was done here, he could go home.

That nest egg he saved was a lot smaller now that he'd also purchased a new apartment. It was his *you're out of debt and officially a grown-up* present to himself. As soon as it was presentable, Jack wanted to have his friends come over for a beer and a cookout. Picturing the guys busting his balls over his new, fancy digs brought a smile to his face.

The majority of his friends still lived up north in Rogers Park and Edgewater in three story walk-ups with roommates. Jack was the first one to move out of the neighborhood; the first one to afford to live by himself. It was undoubtedly going to be weird for the guys.

After placing the last frame atop his desk, he grabbed the leather messenger-style bag his abuela had gifted him with on graduation and walked to the door. Taking one last look at the office, he soaked it all in. His new office.

****

The breeze made the Chicago heat bearable enough to walk the eight blocks home. Popping headphones in and listening to his latest playlist creation which he entitled *Summer Jams*, he walked the tree covered sidewalks. The buildings blended from glass-plated office buildings to steel high-rises with brownstones wedged in between. Jack didn't think he would ever get tired of gazing at the architecture on his regular walks home.

Coming up to his building, he waved to Hank the doorman and walked into the golden lobby. The lobby is actually painted white with gold accents but as the sun sets, the whole space seems to glow. The concierge desk was to the right of the doors and a seating area took over the rest of the space. Past the desk and comfy chairs was the bay of elevators. This was another element that he was going to have to get used to, needing to take an elevator to his apartment on the eighth floor.

The building contained forty floors, the top two taking up the entire floors that belonged to some very famous people—or so he assumed. He didn't actually know who lived up there, but heard rumors of a famous television host, a few political figures and even an Oscar winner ran the gamut. What he did know is that someone needed a special key card to get up there and that the security cameras were abundant on the top floors.

The building also offered a gym, a common area and an outdoor pool, all amenities he hadn't had a chance to touch but planned on it as soon as things slowed down. Looking down at his phone and mentally running thorough his checklist of things to do, out of the corner of one eye, Jack saw a small figure running in his direction.

Charlie, the fluffy Malti-poo who lived two apartments down from him danced down the hallway on his hind legs trying to get his attention. This dog had been all over Jack from the moment he moved in. His owner, the widowed Mrs. Marlow, was a sweet older lady who reminded him of his abuela. Bending down, he gave his new furry friend some love; he asked, "Charlie, where is your mom?"

"Charlie?"

That wasn't the voice of an old woman. His eyes shifted to a pair of white cloth sneakers attached to tan, slim legs. He looked up and took in a sharp breath. A beautiful woman stood in front of him, looking relieved. "Thank you for stopping him. I don't know how I let him get away from me."

Scooping up the dog, Jack took a moment to survey the vision before him. She wore frayed jean shorts and a slouchy white T-shirt that hung off her left shoulder, giving him a glimpse of a light pink bra strap in a shocking contrast against her natural caramel-colored skin. Tousled dark brown hair fell out of a long braid that hung over her right shoulder. A few loose strands fell into her eyes, giving her a frazzled air yet she showed no sign of it on her face. Her full pink lips were set in a smile that went all the way up to her kind brown eyes. Coming to his full height, he took in that she was only a few inches shorter than him yet still had the presence of a tall, willowy dancer.

He couldn't take his eyes off her as he desperately willed his brain to work again. Finally words began to spill out of his mouth. "You're not Mrs. Marlow…"

Her smile widened. "You are very observant. I'm Maddie Conor. I walk Charlie for her. He's usually so well behaved but once we hit the lobby, he just took off rounding the corner…"

As she spoke, her long, tanned fingers seemed to dance in the air. He began to imagine them brushing against his cheek, getting tangled in his hair… Quickly he snapped out of it as the elevator signaled its arrival. "I'm Charlie's neighbor so maybe he recognized my smell? Not that I smell, I mean he's just used to me. Um…but I haven't seen you around before."

Oh God, why could he not be smooth? This woman did not want to hear about his smell, he didn't even smell…at least he didn't think so.

It had been a while since he had been on a date and an even longer time since he'd been in a relationship. The last girlfriend he'd had was at the tail end of law school. Their schedules became hectic, and they ended up drifting apart. Since then, he'd been out and dated but nothing serious or lasting longer than a month at a time. No woman had even piqued his interest enough for him to scale back on work or wouldn't stick around long enough.

For this one, he'd make time…That is if he didn't freak her out with his out of practice flirting first.

Motioning with his free arm for her to move into the elevator, she quickly stepped in, granting him a moment to check out her curvaceous backside. He definitely would have remembered seeing this woman; most definitely, he did not want this to be their only interaction.

"Oh, well, I usually walk him in the afternoons and most people are at work, so I guess our paths wouldn't have crossed yet. Also, you don't have to keep holding him if you don't want."

"Hmm, I don't know, if I put him down you might lose him again and I wouldn't want to get you in trouble with Mrs. Marlow." There it is, this was a normal flirty thing to say.

"Well," she said with a grin, "now that Charlie has identified the exciting smell, I'm sure I can handle him."

"No, no, he's got to be held. I don't want your job to be in jeopardy."

She chuckled. "Thank you for looking out for me…I don't think I caught your name?"

"Jack Delgado. Always here to help a beautiful dog walker."

A faint blush appeared across her cheeks and made his smile grow. He discovered he liked making her blush.

"Well, Jack Delgado, I appreciate it. I should probably take the dog now though."

Their hands brushed as the dog was passed between them. He noticed her sharp intake of breath and felt more certain this attraction was mutual. "Do you always walk him on Friday afternoons? I'm just planning on how early I should leave work next week so that I might run into you again."

The elevator doors opened. Maddie shook her head. "Oh, that's a good line."

Jack couldn't help but throw his head back and bark

out a laugh. This girl was quick.

"You actually have a few more chances to run into me," she said. "Monday, Wednesday, and Friday for the next month I'll be here about this time."

"Oh yeah, what happens next month?"

"I go back to school and mold the minds of Chicago's youth."

"Well then, I guess I have to take a lot more time off before children steal you away."

They approached the door of his neighbor's apartment. His own was two doors away but he made no move to continue on. Before he got a chance to ask for her number, Maddie put the key into the lock. "I guess you will. I look forward to it."

As she slipped through the now open door, and closed it, leaving him standing there, he blew out a breath and scratched the back of his head.

The sound of Mrs. Marlow's doorknob turning made him stop and look. Maddie popped her head out. "Monday, Wednesday, Friday from one thirty to two."

She flashed him a dazzling smile sending a jolt of excitement through his body and hurriedly shut the door again. He smiled and walked back to the door, a new energy in his step.

For once, he was looking forward to a Monday.

Chapter Three

Plans for getting out early on his first "real" day of work proved futile. Monday rolled around and with it, a plethora of case files. On top of that, Jack got pulled into multiple meetings and was made second chair on a few cases. The days blurred and before he knew it, it was lunchtime on Wednesday when he finally stopped to take a breath. Grabbing his wallet, he walked down through the building, heading to Sal's Sandwiches.

"Delgado."

Worried he was somehow in trouble, he turned on the spot and saw Ben Martinez who stood with a gaggle of other uniformed CPD officers. Breaking off from the group, Ben jogged over and gave him a hard hug and clap on the back. "Now that you work here, I'll get to visit more often."

Relieved at the sight of one of his oldest friends in his now familiar uniform, he returned the gesture "Hey man, you here on official business being a big-time policeman or whatever?"

"Yeah." He rolled his eyes and smiled. "Just giving an official statement. It's nice to be inside in air conditioning so I'm trying to drag it out. The heat is nasty out there."

"You been outside all day?"

"You have no idea. There's been a string of robberies and guess who gets to stand outside for crowd control? The latest one was actually right by your place."

"No shit. Maybe I didn't pick the best time to get new digs"

Martinez laughed. "That's what you get for leaving all of us."

Jack shook his head. "I didn't hear you guys complaining this weekend when you drank all my beer…"

"When you invite us all over to build bookshelves, what do you expect?"

They chatted for a few more minutes but that came to an end when one of the cops called out to his friend, signaling it was time for them to head out. Ben left Jack with the promise to come over again on the weekend and drink all his beer again.

Walking into the shop that conveniently had an entrance through the lobby of his office building, Jack thought back to what Ben told him. Wasn't there a streak of robberies in his new neighborhood? How was someone getting into all these high security buildings? Should he get another lock on his door just in case, and maybe one for Mrs. Marlow, too. He didn't want anything to happen to her, or Charlie or…

He checked his watch. He had an hour to get home to possibly see Maddie Conor again. Forgetting lunch, he raced back to his office, determined to get things done so he could fit a walk into his day.

****

I walk slowly through the golden lobby and look over my shoulder toward the door. There is no sign of handsome Jack…again. I thought I would see him on Monday, I even took care to wear a cute little sun dress and fix my hair—but there was no sign of him. Still made an effort with my appearance, wearing a loose, floral tank top and black shorts today. If he doesn't show this time, at least I won't feel dumb for dressing up too much. I even styled my hair, wearing it loose around my shoulders rather than the practical braid I usually go for. I feel dumb thinking he might try to run into me again. It's the middle of the day and he clearly works or is doing things that allow him to afford living in this fancy building.

I lock eyes with Dan, the concierge who is always on duty when I walk Charlie. He gives me a warm smile. "Hiya, Maddie. You doing okay?"

I return the smile and nod. Being a regular, Dan has trusted me with the skeleton key to the building, making it easier and quicker for me to get in and out. We've done this for a few years now. I get the key from him in the beginning of summer and give it back right before Labor Day. I finally stop dawdling and head to the elevator.

The image of Jack in that white collared shirt with the sleeves rolled up and holding a small dog in his arms is seared into my brain. Also, the lopsided grin, the broad shoulders carrying that worn leather messenger bag, the well-toned forearms, his longish dark hair that ended at his stubbled jaw, the details were all there. I could not remember the last time I felt a spark that intense in such a short period of time. Maybe I have been single for too long?

These thoughts swirl around my head as I walk out of the elevator and instantly come to a halt. Leaning against the wall next to Mrs. Marlow's unit is the man who has invaded my thoughts for days.

He is shaking his head in mock disappointment, tsking. "You're late. Your walk was supposedly at one thirty? It's one thirty-three. Poor Charlie is probably dancing with his legs crossed, waiting for you."

I cannot hide the smile that instantly appears on my face. "I'm pretty sure Charlie will forgive me. But I'm not so sure I'll get him to go anywhere with me if you and your scent are standing out here. He won't want to leave."

A slow sexy grin spreads over his chiseled jaw. "Guess I'm just going to have to accompany you on the walk."

"Guess so." I walk up next to him and unlock the door. He smells like sandalwood and despite the air-conditioned hallway, I feel the heat radiating off his body. "We'll be right out." We locked eyes and I felt butterflies awaken inside.

Relieved to escape his presence for a moment, I attempt to pull myself together. Just because this was the first man since Matt to make me feel all warm and tingly does not mean I have to act like a teenager around her first crush. Wrestling the dog into his harness and with a quick glance into the hallway mirror so I can fluff my hair, I slip back out into the hallway.

Walking back out into the warm Chicago air, I lead Jack down the route which Charlie and I usually take. Around the corner, up to the park, cutting through, and back down a parallel street. We slowly amble down the sidewalk with an excited Charlie sniffing everything in sight.

"So, what job do you have where you can just leave and go on a walk in the middle of the day?"

My abruptness brings the grin back to his face. "I'm a lawyer with The People's Law Collective. I had a light workload today, but I also brought stuff home. I just started last week which is why I didn't get the chance to casually run into you on Monday."

"And here I was thinking you forgot about me," I tease, keeping my tone light.

Jack looks up and catches my eye. "I don't think that's possible."

I feel the blush creep into my cheeks and look down. I won't deny I am flattered. "Another very good line. But it makes sense, now that I know you're a lawyer, you've probably got a million charming things to say."

He lets out a loud laugh, and I hide a small smile; I like making him laugh. "No, I promise I don't. A lot of guys at the place where I used to work ran along those lines, but I wasn't one of them, I swear."

"Oh, so you used to be around the swanky guys?"

Laughing again, he answers, "Yes. We defended a lot of white-collar cases, but I've always wanted to work for the people who really need it."

My heart beats a little faster. How could this man get any more perfect? He continues, "But hey, you're the expert on helping people. I mean, a teacher? I could never do that."

"Yeah, it's not the easiest, but it is fun. I always end up loving my kids, even the ones who make me want to rip my hair out. I guess it's also nice that we get a break for the summer, too. I mean if I'm not walking dogs, I'm pretty much sitting on my balcony with a book and a cold drink."

"Oh, that sounds like the life. I haven't really been out on my balcony here yet but at my previous place we had a big backyard where we would do small bonfires and play games. It was the best."

We continue talking about the neighborhoods we

live in, the food we like, and television we watch. I am surprised how much I enjoy the conversation, never finding an awkward moment or uncomfortable pause. As we round the final corner, I realize our walk is coming to an end and start to get bummed out. I don't want the afternoon to end.

Suddenly sirens are blaring and I jump, looking over my shoulder. Cop cars appear out of nowhere, coming to a stop at a building down the block. Charlie plants himself on the sidewalk, barking at the noise. Distracted and not looking where I am going; a strong, warm hand on my lower back suddenly pulls me back from the curb before I step off. Turning, I find my face inches from Jack's.

Immediately, my senses are overloaded. Another waft of sandalwood surrounds me, and I study his face up close. His bronzed skin hides the beginnings of crow's feet around his eyes. This is a man whose smile seems to always reach his eyes. The brown irises have flecks of green that give off a warmth. His dark hair, thicker than I first realized, blows across his face, slightly obscuring his mouth. I am acutely aware of his hand, still on my back, holding me close.

"That was close." His voice comes out rough, causing me to let go of the breath I didn't realize I was holding. My chest rises rapidly causing his gaze to momentarily dip down, then back up. We both laugh and he quickly lets me go, much to my disappointment.

As we turn into the golden lobby with Charlie heading the charge for the elevators, Jack clears his throat. "There's been a bunch of robberies down here. I bet that building got hit."

"I actually heard about that on *Murder for Your*

Thoughts, this crime podcast I listen to all the time."

"You're one of those girls? Serial killer documentaries and blogs?" The teasing tone from before comes back into his voice.

"Yup. Keeps me vigilant. They help me determine whether a cute guy is actually going to murder me."

We walk into the elevator and rather than standing on opposite sides of the small area, Jack stands right next to me. "So you're saying I'm cute?" His fingers suddenly brush my hair back over my shoulder. "You shouldn't hide that smile."

I look at him, and for a brief moment think he might lean in and kiss me. I hear the blood pounding in my ears and force myself not to fidget. Do I want him to kiss me? I mean I just met this guy.

Ding.

The elevator doors open on the eighth floor; I am literally saved by the bell. We both take a breath and smile at each other as we walk out into the hallway.

"Thanks for letting me join your walk today."

I put a little extra something into my smile. "Charlie and I were both happy to have the company."

We get to the door, and I begin to dawdle with the key to Mrs. Marlow's apartment. I don't want to leave him. Jack stares at the floor as he shifts his feet. "Um, yeah it was fun."

I stare at him as he continues to avoid eye contact. I need to put him out of his misery. "Would you like to go on another walk with me? Possibly one that happens at night? Maybe going to and from a place that serves food? Also, Charlie wouldn't be there."

He laughs, finally looking up with a relieved smile. "I would love to."

He has returned to his confident self as I put my number in his phone. He quickly leans in to kiss my cheek, and my heart flutters as he lingers a moment longer…and then Charlie barks. Apparently, he is tired of just hanging out in the hallway.

Saying my good-byes, I slip inside to take care of Charlie. Before I left, I felt my phone vibrate with a text message.

—Tomorrow at 7? —

I smile, sending back a thumbs up emoji. Feeling excited, I immediately text Sarah and Stephanie. We are about to spend the night, trying on every bit of clothing I own.

Chapter Four

"Thank God I taught you how to be charming. Otherwise, showing up like a stalker at the door waiting for her could've been taken as really creepy."

Jack shook his head, throwing the bottle cap from his beer at Mike as the rest of his friends chuckled. Mike, Ben, Marcus, and Stevie, his oldest friends, sat in ancient lawn chairs in a semicircle in Mike's backyard. This was their tradition; a weekly debrief in someone's yard, polishing off a case of beer and spending way too much money at the taco place around the corner. Jack just finished telling them all about Maddie. And of course, Mike has something to say about it.

Marcus sat up straighter, gesturing wildly with his bottle. "You taught him to be charming? If I remember correctly, I was the one who played wingman for him when he finally asked out Layla Giardin in high school."

Ever since middle school, Marcus and Mike grew up as neighbors and therefore, each knew exactly what to say to push each other's buttons.

Jack looked over at Ben who just smirked and took another pull of his drink as those two kept arguing. The quietest of the bunch, Ben Martinez was always the one to sit back and observe, not get involved before having all the details. It's what made him a good cop. Jack may have been the first one to leave the neighborhood, but he knew Ben was on the way out, too. He was working his way up in the force to become a detective and with his help on busting a kidnapper in a high-profile case last year, he was close to becoming one of the youngest detectives on the force. He chose to work in a precinct downtown, and with him plugging in more and more hours, sooner or later, he was bound to leave the neighborhood and move closer to Jack.

Movement from the corner of his eye broke him out of these thoughts as he saw Stevie moving his chair from the sun to a shady patch. "Why are we out here again? I mean, now that we know someone with air conditioned rooms and a balcony and probably a pool or some shit?"

Jack raised his hands in defense. "You guys were there last week and bitched about the commute. I think I remember you specifically saying *there's one of you and four of us so it's easier if you come to us.*"

Stevie was the youngest of the group. The cousin of Ben and a year younger than the rest of the guys, he basically grew into the role of little brother. Jack specifically had been called by him numerous times over the years to help him out of situations he'd gotten himself into. Even though he drove him crazy, Jack would still have done anything for him.

Stevie looked away pursing his lips, "I don't remember any of this, so don't use your lawyer mind tricks on me—"

Jack snorted. "Those *mind tricks* are called memories."

Stevie playfully *tsk'ed,* dismissing this answer, as he opened another beer. He tipped it toward Jack, "Seriously, a new place and a new girl? Congrats, man."

The rest of the group copied him and tilted their bottles in Jack's direction. Shaking his head, he replied,

"Nah, I don't have a new girl…not yet at least."

"If you keep up this creeper routine, you will soon," Mike teased.

Ben leaned in. "Please don't be creepy, I don't wanna have to arrest you."

Mirroring him, Jack leaned in, smacked his arm with the back of his hand, surprising himself when he was left with sore knuckles. "Jesus, Ben. Working out much?" He flexed his fingers, trying to shake out the pain.

Ben shrugged and swallowed his sip. "Or want me to check her out? Make sure she's worth creeping on?"

Marcus pointed an accusing bottle in Ben's direction. "Isn't that an abuse of power?"

Ben shrugged. "Chicago is a big city with lots of crime. Everyone is a suspect. I'm sure I can figure something out."

Draining his drink, Jack snatched the bottle from his friend's hand, then stood and stretched. "Leave her alone, no *checking out* necessary. I'm taking her out to dinner tonight, so I'll be doing the checking out myself. Now I didn't come all the way up here to just see your ugly faces. I need some shredded pork tacos and I need it now."

****

"That was very sneaky of you."

Jack and I had just finished dinner and drinks at Chance, a cozy restaurant in Wicker Park. When I had asked for the check, the smirking waiter told me it had already been taken care of.

"I really wanted to show off my spy skills and I thought that would be a good start."

He catches up to me and we both stroll at a slow pace, making no certain moves on where to go next. He's wearing a pair of dark jeans and a light blue shirt and looks damn good. The buttons on his shirt, done up halfway, left a peek of chest hair which makes him somehow more attractive. All through dinner I had to keep reminding myself to stop ogling him.

He grabs my hand, entwining our fingers, and my heart flutters all over again. You'd think I would never have held hands before. "Since I picked the place for dinner, would you want to pick a bar and grab a drink? I mean I could but since you actually live over here, I'm assuming you have some good recommendations."

I start listing off a few places that are within walking distance and Jack picks a dive bar known as The Hatch. I hesitate for a moment but thankfully he doesn't notice. It's too late now; The Hatch is a favorite haunt of my ex, Matt.

He broke up with me a couple months ago and looking back, I regret not doing it first. He is a scheduler for Ruffin' It, the dog walking service where we both work. When we first met, I fell head over heels for him. He's tall with blond, close-cropped hair and blue eyes. He looked like he would be a football player and prom king and he had the charm to go along with it. We flirted pretty hard for the first few years when I finally let my guard down and agreed to go out with him.

For the most part, it was a nice relationship. Matt was easy on the eyes, fun, funny and nice to my parents. It wasn't long before I fell in love. Pretty soon after I told him I loved him, he became distant. He would tease me to the point of actually hurting my feelings. Then he became unpleasant and began to hang around a group of guys who gave off a weird vibe. Sarah and Stephanie sat me down at one point to tell me what they were seeing. I defended him, of course, saying work was stressful, and money was tight for him.

Not even a week later, he asked me to go on a walk around the park and told me our relationship was over, stating we wanted different things. He then left me standing there and walked off, leaving me to sob by myself. I walked home where Sarah and Steph practically carried me upstairs and into bed. I wallowed for one day before I realized how badly he treated me and never looked back.

Of course, that didn't make it easier for those times when I ran into him at work. Even last week when I ran into the office to pick up my check, he still has some sort of smug manner to him. He would look at me, with an almost pitying look, and I couldn't stand it.

"Maddie?"

I snap back to the present as Jack, with a puzzled expression on his face, gives my hand a squeeze. "Oh yeah, I'm sorry, I was just…trying to remember the last time I was there."

He didn't look convinced. "Do you want to go somewhere else?"

I give him a smile and resume a normal walking speed. "No, no, it's right up the street, let's go."

We get to the bar and before we can go inside, the door swings open and three men exit the place. In a city of 2.7 million people, the one person I didn't want to see walks out at the exact time I arrive. *What did I do for this type of karmic intervention?*

"Oh crap," I mutter under my breath as I look around, hoping Matt doesn't recognize me.

Jack turns to me as we stop walking. "Maddie?"
Was it too late to hide behind something?

"Oh dang, Maddie, it is you. What's up?"

Before I can say anything, Matt takes two huge steps toward me, wrapping me in a hug that I do not return. I feel Jack's hand leave my back for the briefest moment as I'm tugged toward my ex-boyfriend, and I miss the warmth and security I didn't realize it provided. When it's clear that I am not responding, Matt unwinds his arms and takes a step back toward his friends, leaving the smell of his cheap cologne all over my shirt.

He's wearing an open collared shirt with a tight, black T-shirt underneath and cargo shorts. Had he always looked like a jackass? His other two friends are dressed in a similar fashion, looking like his clones. I guess the douche-ness inside him attracted these two. It looks like they're traveling in a pack.

Jack must feel I'm not happy because he lets go of my hand and moves his to the small of my back. His drawing me closer to his side does not go unnoticed by Matt.

"Matt, I forgot you come here. This is Jack…" I clearly don't know how to finish this sentence or this conversation.

One of Matt's eyebrows rise and a small smile comes to his lips, which sets off warning bells in my mind. "I remember I used to bring you here all the time when we dated. Remember that time you drank so much that I basically had to carry you home? Or maybe you wouldn't remember that."

I hate him. I hate his stupid smug face. "I actually do remember that. You guilted me into finishing a bunch of drinks that I didn't even order because you said money was tight. It was very classy of you."

Jack's hand momentarily tightens around my waist,

then eases up. His thumb begins to slowly move in a circle over my side, melting all my tension and replacing it with a heat that I didn't expect. I turn my attention to him, lightly placing my hand on his shoulder and lean in. "Wanna keep walking?"

He gives me a big smile. "Absolutely." Then, he turns to Matt. "— Mike, was it? Great meeting you."

Without waiting for a reply, he pulls me away from the door and we begin to walk down the street. His hand drifts slightly lower down my back making me giggle. I look at him out the side of my eye, he smiles at me like he knows what I'm thinking.

"I'm just following your lead," he murmurs. "He's going to hate seeing this."

If it meant pissing Matt off I guess I could let Jack touch any part of me.

We make it another block before I look back over my shoulder. Matt and his friends are nowhere to be seen. Jack's hand leaves its spot, albeit slowly, and makes its way back to my hand. I tug on it gently, leading him toward the entrance of the park across the street. We start taking the path, slowly making our way around.

"So that was your ex I take it?"

"Oh, could you tell?"

He chuckles, waiting a beat before he continues. "I wanted to say something but I figured you wouldn't want me to beat the crap out of that guy on our first date."

My head swivels in surprise at the admission. I didn't take him for a violent guy, but I'm also touched and honestly, slightly turned on, at the idea of him defending me so aggressively, and after only one date. "He's not worth bruising your knuckles over."

By now, his thumb is tracing circles over my hand

and I'm imagining him doing more with those fingers and…Wow I have to calm down.

"I think you're pretty great," he says. "I wouldn't mind bruising my knuckles for you."

Taken aback by the flattery, I don't look where I'm stepping and trip, but his reflexes are quick. His other hand shoots out, catching me about the waist and I find myself reminded of the last time we were in the position, face to face. It seems he does, too.

"We keep finding ourselves like this. I'm starting to think you're doing it on purpose."

I let out a breathless laugh, all too focused on how close his lips are to mine. My eyes dart up to his and I feel my insides turning to jelly from the heat of his gaze. He lets go of my hand, bringing it up toward my cheek and cupping my face softly. "I…"

There is that hesitation again; him going ninety percent of the way and waiting for me to fill in the last part. What's happened to make him so hesitant?

Immediately, I close the gap and our lips connect. I can feel his surprise at first, but it quickly disappears as his hand moves from my cheek to the back of my head. His other hand moves to my lower back, and he pulls me close. My hands find their way up to his hair. It's softer than I imagined. I just want to spend hours playing with it. Without thought, I open my mouth, letting him take the kiss deeper. I love the feeling of his stubble scraping my cheeks, the contrast of the rough cheek and soft lips is amazing. I'm now pressed against his body and can feel how hard and muscular he is. My left hand drifts down to his shoulder and my nails involuntarily dig into him as his tongue finds its way into my mouth. I'm now practically molded into him, but he doesn't seem to mind as his hand on my lower back keeps me firmly in place.

I can't remember the last time I was kissed like this. I'm hungry for his mouth, and I can't get enough of it. Suddenly I feel a pressure against my hip and realize he's getting turned on too. My mind begins to click back on, reminding me that we're in a very public park, which happens to be in a neighborhood where I know people. On top of that, we're standing in the middle of the sidewalk for everyone to see.

I move both my hands to his chest and begin to lightly push and our mouths reluctantly separate. I feel lightheaded and embarrassed that I'm panting, only to realize he is too. I look up at him and he gives me a lazy smile, lust still fogging his eyes. He clears his throat. "I'm…uh…sorry. I think I got carried away."

I feel my eyes go wide. "No, no I'm sorry. I kind of just attacked you with my face…"

We both nervously laugh and look down; his arms are still wrapped around me. He slowly extricates himself and backs away, running his hands through his hair. "I swear, that's not how I normally do a first kiss."

"Me neither," I say and quickly add, "why don't you walk me home before we get arrested for public indecency?"

That earns me a genuine laugh. We walk in silence for a few moments, trying to collect ourselves. I try to subtly look at his crotch to see if what I felt was actually there but it's way too dark now. His hand finds mine again and we walk, now in a comfortable silence, back to my apartment.

Once we arrive outside my building, Jack turns to me. "I think this could go without saying but I really like you and would like to see you again."

"I was thinking the same thing."

This time, there is no hesitation. He closes the space between us, cradling my face with both hands, and plants a soft, sweet kiss on my lips. He ends it just as fast and takes a step back, shoving his hands in his back pockets. "Now that we're on your street, I figured we should keep it PG."

I laugh and say goodbye as I turn and walk up the steps to my building. Before I slip through the door, I look back over my shoulder to see he hasn't moved and is still grinning at me. I walk up the stairs, and for the rest of the night, I'm sure I have the biggest smile plastered on my face.

Chapter Five

The next week and a half seem to fly by. Mostly it's because I can't stop thinking about Jack. Since that night, we have texted nonstop, and he joined Charlie and me for a walk a few more times. We have a date planned for tonight, and I'm feeling slightly nervous about being alone with him. On top of texting him almost nonstop, I can't stop thinking about that kiss.

Something happened when our lips connected but I'm not quite sure what. Whatever it was made me lose control, which has never happened before. Based on what he said after the kiss, it wasn't a normal occurrence for him either.

As I travel to my last dog walk of the day, which happens to be in his building because it's Charlie, my hand drifts up to my cheek. When I recall the feel of his facial hair against my skin, heat pools at my core.

As I pass the reception desk, I look up and see Dan, the regular attendant, there along with two other men. One of them looks familiar but I'm not sure why. They must be new, getting trained or something. They all look up and nod at me as I pass, and I go back into my daydreams.

When the elevator doors open and I walk out, it takes me a moment to realize I've gone to the wrong floor, twelve instead of eight. Cursing myself for my spaciness, I turn around and press the button for the elevator again. As I wait, I hear the sound of a cart behind me. Turning, I see a maintenance worker rolling a cart toward me and immediately I'm alert.

He's an older man, probably around sixty, wearing gray coveralls and a set of keys on his belt loop. Nothing about his stance or distance should send warning bells, but his eye contact is giving me bad vibes. He's staring at me as if I bothered him. Attempting to lighten the mood, I give him a small smile and jump a little as the elevator doors finally open.

Rushing inside, I put my arm out holding the doors open and ask, "Going down?"

He shakes his head slightly and continues to stare as I drop my arm and let the doors close on him. I sag against the back wall and shiver, trying to shake off whatever that weird interaction was. Instead, I turn my thoughts to happier things, mainly Jack.

These thoughts follow me all the way down to Mrs. Marlow's apartment. It takes me a few tries to wrangle Charlie into his harness, I'm so distracted. I catch my reflection in the mirror as we leave. I have that dopey grin on my face again. I shake my head and try my hardest to concentrate on the dog for the next half hour.

As I get to the park, my phone buzzes with a text from Jack.

—How's Charlie today? —

I know it's not exactly difficult to remember my dog-walking schedule, especially when he has joined a few times, but I love that he remembers.

—He's good but he definitely felt bummed when you weren't waiting outside his door today—

—Oh? Was it just him who was bummed or is he just picking up on the feelings of his walker? —

I snort. His confidence still astounds me.

—*Nope, definitely just him. He told me. I speak dog, didn't you know?* —

—*Ah, ok. Just wanted to double check. Can you tell him that I wish I was there rather than work? Also tell him that I'm sorry I can't hang out with him tonight as I have plans with this amazing lady—*

I shake my head and smile.

—*Oh I'll let him know, gotta tell him that I too have plans with this hot lawyer—*

—*So you think I'm hot...but seriously about tonight, would you mind if we changed the time?—*

We are out of the park now, coming up on the building. This time, the walk with Charlie has become a bit longer, as I keep stopping to text Jack. The dog doesn't seem to mind. He's too busy sniffing. Jack and I were supposed to meet tonight at seven. Seeing as this is the last job I have today; I don't mind, and I tell him so.

He responds:

—*Good, so you don't mind if we start earlier? Say...now?—*

My brows knit as I reread what he just sent. All of a sudden, the leash starts to move. Charlie is pulling away like a mad dog.

I look up to see Jack walking toward us, a grin on his face. He looks so good in his tight button-up shirt with the sleeves rolled up. His hair, which I assume was brushed back this morning, is loose around his face and his amber eyes are alight with mischief.

I loosen my hold on the dog as soon as Jack is near enough so Charlie can attack him with kisses. He bends to give the dog some attention and looks up at me, smile still in place. "Did you like what I did there with the texting and the appearing? Pretty romantic huh?"

I laugh and see his smile widen. He stands up and leans in to give me a kiss on the cheek. Ever since that night, we've had an unspoken agreement to keep it rated PG on our walks. I inhale his cologne and feel my chest tighten as he lingers for a moment. When will I be able to get close to him without getting butterflies in my tummy? Hell, when will I be able to smell a sandalwood-based cologne again without my insides running rampant? His eyes narrow as he pulls away. He definitely knows he has an effect on me.

I clear my throat. "So you snuck out of work?" He falls into step next to me, our arms brushing against one another. "No, I'm just so good at my job that I was able to finish early. Well, that and the fact that I stayed late practically all week to make sure I was free tonight."

I look at him, my eyes wide with surprise. He does not seem annoyed or mad about it, and I am touched he would do that, just to see me. "I don't really know what to say to that."

He feigns surprise, pulling me to a stop. "What? I've finally made you speechless? You, who always has at least two comebacks ready?"

I lift my hand to smack his arm, but he catches it midair, laughing. He slides his hand into mine and we continue walking. I'm looking at him as we round the final corner but I am immediately distracted by the police cars in front of Jack's building, drawing the usual crowd of onlookers. I look back at Jack and see he's as confused as I am. We pick up the pace.

"You didn't go home before you met up with me and Charlie, did you?"

"No, but if this is what I think it is…" He trails off

when we reach the crowd, his eyes scanning for someone specific. We make our way to the front of the small crowd to the doors only to be stopped by a policeman asking if we lived in the building.

As we start to explain, I see a familiar face over his shoulder through the open doors to the lobby. "Jenny?"

A blonde head turns toward me, and I see her beautiful face look somewhat relieved but streaked with tears. Seeing this, the officer lets Jack and me pass him into the now buzzing lobby.

Jenny is a young mother of two adorable boys and a big German shepherd named Benny that I walk from time to time. Luckily Jack has scooped up Charlie because when we get close, Jenny practically throws herself into my arms. "I'm glad to see a familiar face."

I give her a reassuring pat on the back but then quickly pull away. "Oh my God, Jenny. Are the boys all right?"

She nods vehemently. "Yes, they're at day camp right now, thank God. I just ran out to the store for ten minutes, when someone broke into our apartment." Her tears begin to spill down her cheeks. "Benny tried to bite whoever it was and got shoved into the bathroom. The dog's okay but our place is just wrecked."

I lean in and give her another hug, knowing this is all I can do, and turn my head to look at Jack whose expression is grim.

"There's been a string of home invasions lately. I was hoping it would skip our building," he says. Jenny pulls out of my embrace, her attention being grabbed by another officer.

Jack scans the room, this time finding who he was looking for. "Ben."

I follow his gaze and see a shorter, tanned man with dark hair look up. He makes his way toward us, his hands tucked inside his vest. Upon first glance, he looks relaxed and at ease but his eyes survey the entire area, alert for anything. "Jack, what are you doing home so early? And did you get a dog?"

We all look down at Charlie who is still in Jack's arms, wagging his tail at all the attention he is suddenly getting. I reach to grab him. Jack chuckles and relinquishes the fluffy dog. "No, no this is my neighbor's dog and this is Maddie, my…um…"

He looks at me as he trails off and I can't blame him. I don't really know what our label is yet, or if we even needed one. I jump in. "I'm the dog walker and also his friend and…um…date for tonight."

Recognition seems to wash over the man's face. "Oh, this is the girl you've been talking about."

I feel my cheeks flush as I look back at Jack. He looks at me with a half-smile. "Yeah, this is her."

This Ben, or whatever his name is, breaks out into a grin and offers me his hand. "It's great to meet you. I'm Ben Martinez, pretty much his best friend since forever. From what I hear, you're the greatest thing since sliced bread."

Gosh there must be something in the water where they grew up because now that he's smiling, I can see Ben is just as hot as Jack. Jack shakes his head. I'm pretty sure I hear him mutter something to his friend about killing him. Unfortunately, he changes the topic before I can pry more into what else was said about me.

"So do you think this is the same group?"

Ben's expression switches back to serious as he turns to Jack. "Definitely. So, you got to be careful."

"Are they breaking in or picking the locks on these doors?" I ask.

Looking surprised, both men turn to me. "Um, they pick the locks," Ben says. "So, adding more locks or more high-tech ones to the doors will either slow them down enough to be caught or deter them completely."

"They've definitely been watching the buildings since most of them happen during the day when everyone is at work," I said. "They probably know when the apartments are empty. And the apartments themselves, is there some sort of calling card that links it to the same group over and over?"

Ben crosses his arms and glances at Jack then back at me. "They smash all the mirrors—a lot. Like, overkill."

"And quite frankly annoying" Jack says. "Those big mirrors in the bathrooms must cost a bunch…" I smirk at him and he smiles back.

"Did you install extra locks?" Ben asks.

Jack shakes his head. "Not yet, and I need to bring over the other to Mrs. Marlow's apartment."

My heart beats a little faster when I hear this. He bought an extra lock for his elderly neighbor. Oh boy, I can feel my hormones kick into high gear.

"Maybe I should talk to management about sending out a memo or something. Maddie," he asks, turning to me, "does Jenny have lots of locks on the door?"

Before I can answer, Ben asks, "You know the victim?"

I shrug my shoulders. "I've walked her dog before. You know what's weird, I actually was on her floor earlier today. Everything looked normal."

Ben's attention is still on me. "Why were you up

there? It's not the same floor as Jack's."

"Oh I accidentally hit the wrong button, just being spacy. I ended up seeing a kind of creepy janitor guy, but I didn't think too much of it."

Ben is silent for a minute, mulling over my words. "Do you only walk dogs in this building?"

I shake my head.

"What about the Elliot or the Davis?"

I'm confused by his mention of other buildings in the area. "Well, I've had assignments in both places before but not as regularly as this one."

"And you get the key…?"

These questions, coming in quick succession are starting to make me feel uncomfortable. "I get the key from the front desk."

Before he can ask another question, Jack jumps in. "Hey, Ben, what's with the third degree?"

He shrugs nonchalantly. "Just curious."

Jack's hand moves protectively to my lower back, his eyes still on Ben. They seem to be having some sort of silent conversation, and it's definitely about me. I clear my throat and look up. "I better be getting Charlie back home. It was nice to meet you, Ben."

I give him a smile and he returns the friendly gesture but this time the smile doesn't reach his eyes. "I'll see you around, Jack." He nods at his friend then turns and goes back to a group of officers.

Without waiting, I walk through the busy lobby to the elevators, Jack on my heels. Neither of us speaks until we get into the waiting elevator and the doors close. "This is a little crazy," I tell him. "I mean, everything was normal a half hour ago when I arrived. They even had extra help today so I'm not sure how this happened."

"Extra help?"

I look up into Jack's green-flecked eyes. "Yeah, there were like three guys behind the desk today. I think they're training or something." Then my imagination starts to run wild. "Oh, what if that was a cover?"

Jack's eyebrows furrow, like he's not understanding me, so I continue. "Maybe they were casing the joint."

His features smooth out in amusement. "I'm sorry, were they criminals from New York in the 20s?"

"No, seriously, think about it. New guys on the same day as a robbery? Text Ben about it and tell him it's my theory."

Jack smirks but nods his head and silently wraps his arms around me. I lean into him, my free arm snaking around his waist and close my eyes for a moment. The comfort is short-lived as we arrive at our destination. "I wish you lived on a higher floor," I grumble.

We stand in the hallway and make plans on where to grab food. Afterward, I slip inside the Marlow apartment and let Charlie off the leash. I stand up and look around, an uneasy feeling in my stomach. What if someone tried to break in here?

I shake the thought out of my head and let myself out, thoughts shifting to dinner and Jack's amber eyes.

Chapter Six

Jack was buried in files, or at least that was what his desk made it look like. The weekend came and went quickly. Now, being back in the office, everyone wanted his opinion or help on their cases. He finished a note, closed the file, and added it to a dangerously tall pile in the *done* box. Leaning back, he rolled his shoulders and stretched, wishing he was able to take a walk with Maddie today.

Maddie.

The memory of her laughing during dinner on Friday made him smile. He had taken her to a little café around the corner from his building and they stayed until the waiters practically ushered them out the door. They talked about everything and nothing and there was never a moment of boredom. He could listen to stories about her teaching for hours and be happy. He figured he could just sit in silence with her and be happy.

Afterward, he walked her to the bus stop. He tried calling her a taxi, but she insisted on taking the bus. Thinking back, maybe she just wanted to spend more time with him as they waited on the bench at the stop. He ended up kissing her goodnight but made sure it was nowhere near as…passionate as that first night. Jack even waited to see the bus, so he had an honest-to-God excuse to pull away but, God was it hard. It also did not help satiate his growing need for her. It actually took him a moment after the bus pulled away to be able to get up and walk home. It was embarrassing, to some degree, that lust alone for this woman could do that to him. He theorized that maybe they just needed to be alone, in an apartment, and get it out of their systems? Then maybe he wouldn't feel the need to practically paw at her every time they got close—

The sudden ringing of his office phone pulled him out of his thoughts. Getting back into his professional mindset, he answered brusquely, "Delgado."

He was greeted with a phony, nasal voice saying, "Um yes, Mr. Delgado? I have a Ben Martinez on the line for you."

He didn't fool me. "Ben, are you pretending you're important enough to have a secretary make your calls?"

His laugh filled the receiver. "Pretending? Psh, I run this place."

"Ha, so what's up, bud?"

Gone was the congenial tone as he said, "I actually wanted to talk to you about those robberies."

"Have you gotten any leads?"

"No, but I was thinking…I mean I know this is random, but I was thinking about Maddie."

As Jack waited for him to continue, an uneasy feeling bloomed in his gut.

"Just that she has been to a lot of the places where the robbers hit—"

Jack cut him off. "Let me stop you there. If you're about to say what I think you're going to say then—"

He rushed into his reply. "No, no I'm not saying anything, but it just seems curious right? Or a really big coincidence. Maybe it's someone like her, a dog walker or a delivery man or someone who has casual access to all these buildings. You got to admit that. Plus, I mean, you seem really into her and that's great, but it just makes me think, how much do you really know about her?"

"Ben," Jack warned, "I know plenty about her. She's a teacher and walks dogs to make a little extra money. She is not a criminal mastermind. She actually listens to true crime podcasts. I'm one hundred percent certain she'd rather solve a crime than commit it."

"But she's choosing these pricy areas and—"

"Yeah, because she makes more money, not because she's casing apartments."

"Okay, okay, I'm sorry. This is just so coincidental. I really didn't mean to make you upset man."

His knuckles turned white as his grip on the phone tightened. Forcing himself to relax, he took a breath. "No, I get it. I mean, I understand how your mind works. Oh—" He straightened as he remembered. "—I forgot. Maddie actually wanted me to text you. She said they had extra help behind the lobby desk in my building that day. Thinks they hired new people and are training them or something? Or look into that creepy janitor she mentioned, or I don't know…" Jack trailed off, feeling agitated and flustered.

"I'll go back and look over the notes."

There was a silence on the other end of the phone and Jack imagined his friend just nodding his head in agreement. He finally spoke again, "Just keep an eye out for anything, okay? Even if it's something weird."

He sighed. "I will. Thanks."

Hanging up, his head dropped into his hands, massaging his temples as he tried to abate the growing anger. The speed at which he jumped to her defense surprised him, but it spoke to how strong of a connection he'd formed with her in the short time they'd known each other. He didn't want his friend to think ill of her, he wanted him to like her. He wanted to bring her to a party and have a beer with the group and for all of them to nod and smile in approval, and he wanted Maddie to want that too. It was that uncertainty that made him continue to hesitate when they got close or too intimate, but she encouraged him every time. *She's not like the others; she's going to be around for a long time.*

Checking his watch, he saw that it was time for lunch and a well-deserved break. Grabbing his wallet, he opened the door only to have a small fist smack him in the face. Uttering a string of colorful words that probably should not be heard in the office, his hands flew to his face. "Oh my God, I'm so sorry. I was knocking as you opened, I'm so, so sorry."

He knew that voice. Dropping his left hand while massaging the bridge of his nose with his right, he saw Maddie standing there. She wore a sleeveless mint green dress and brown strappy sandals. She pinned her hair back away from her face with the rest tumbling down her back and adorning her arms were her normal smattering of silver bangles. Her hands covered her mouth and a look of horror plastered over her face.

Jack immediately laughed and then groaned as the movement increased the soreness in his face. Her hands slid up, covering her entire face as she said, "What is wrong with me?"

Jack's hands flew to hers and pried them away from her beautiful face. "It's really okay, it was more a surprise than it was painful. Look, I won't even get a bruise, I promise."

Her eyes, wide and round as saucers, still filled with

worry. "Are you sure?"

He grinned and nodded in confirmation, the pain subsiding. This granted him a relieved smile and he looked down at his hands holding hers. Her skin felt so soft, he couldn't help but run his thumbs along her palms. Wait…

"Wait, what are you doing here?"

Her relieved smile turned into a knowing one. "I wanted to surprise you. I unexpectedly have the afternoon free and was wondering if you wanted to grab lunch unless…"

She trailed off as she glanced behind him. He followed her gaze realizing the organized mess of his desk looked a lot different to her than it did in his head

Chuckling, he said, "No, most of that is actually finished. I swear. Also, that was perfect timing, I was literally leaving to go get food. Well, until I was attacked in my own doorway that is."

Her hands flew back up to her eyes, covering her embarrassment. "I'm sorry."

Laughing, he again pried them away from her face. This time, her warm brown eyes held humor in them.

"Where exactly did I hit you?" Inhaling her vanilla and lavender scent, he pointed to the bridge of his nose. She gently placed her hands on either side of his face and lifted up onto her toes. "Should I kiss it and make it better?"

He felt the muscles in his core tighten. Not trusting his own voice, he simply nodded. She leaned in as he closed his eyes and planted the softest kiss on the bridge of his nose. As quick as it happened, he felt her start to lower down onto her heels and he mourned her absence.

Finally finding his voice, in an almost hoarse

whisper he said, "You have no idea how much better I feel now."

He opened his eyes and caught her staring at him with mischief. Slowly remembering lunch, he reluctantly began to pull back when an idea occurred. Wasn't he just thinking how he wanted to be alone with her? Looking to his left at the small, black leather couch which thankfully was not covered in files, he turned back and asked, "How hungry are you?"

****

Those green flecks seem to be swirling in his eyes as he asks the question, raising his eyebrow. "Um...I mean, I can wait a bit. Why? Are you going to give me a tour?"

"I was thinking of giving you a tour but mainly of my office." Without waiting for an answer, he pulls my hands, which he is still holding, sending me stumbling through the door and into his arms.

Grinning down at me, he reaches around and closes the door, locking it. I raise my eyebrows and he feigns innocence. "I'm officially on lunch now, I don't want anyone else coming in asking me to do something. I've got a particularly important lunch date."

I smile and he moves in closer but I'm still feeling rather embarrassed about the fist to the face and dodge his advance. Swiftly stepping to the side, I gesture around the room. "So, all this is yours, huh? I'll need a very in-depth tour." He blows out a breath and chuckles. A sly smile spreads across his lips as he plays along. "Well, why don't we start with the view?"

I walk over to the window and look out. His window overlooks LaSalle Street. We're up on the fifth floor, and I have to lean my head against the glass to get a view of the sidewalk down below. Directly across the narrow street is a glass building that is so shiny I can almost make out our reflections. I see a shape walk up to what I assume is mine in the reflective glass. Without turning my head, I ask, "Do you know what offices are across the street from you?"

I feel his hot breath against the side of my face as he says in a low voice, "I think that's an empty space right now."

My fingers curl in, nails biting my palms. I breathe in, my chest swelling, I can hear his sharp intake of breath and I know he's looking straight down my dress. Turning my head, his eyes snap back up to mine as I look at him from underneath my eyelashes. My voice comes out huskier than intended when I say, "Well, that's convenient. There's no one to watch what's going on in here."

He swallows hard, and I slowly grin and push against the window, backing away from it and raising my voice to its normal tone. "What else?"

I walk to his desk and feel him following right behind me. His arms surround me, palms landing on the desk on either side of me. His waist pushes me up against the desk, my body trapped between him and the furniture.

"This is where I do important lawyer things as you can tell." He grabs a handful of folders, pushing them into a pile, clearing off a small space on the desk. "Sorry let me just clean up a bit."

His head nuzzles my temple as he places his chin on my shoulder. His left-hand drifts to my waist, his fingers begin to graze up and down my side, the thin fabric of my dress doing nothing to stop the warmth of his skin on mine. I angle my face toward him, and in an instant his lips are on mine. His right hand flies up to the side of my face, holding me in place as his lips devour mine. A gasp escapes my mouth, and he takes the chance, moving his tongue in. I feel my body begin to lean back into his and before I can turn, he's gone, walking to the other side of the desk.

He swings his head around, lips swollen. "The tour continues over here, when you're ready."

I realize my mouth is hanging open in disbelief of his abrupt departure from my side and I quickly shut it. I feel the blood rush to my cheeks and heat rush straight down through my core. I slowly walk around the desk, my fingers tracing the edge of the wood. His eyes are fixated on my hands. I brush past him, making sure my hands softly graze his chest, and sit on the leather couch behind him. The skirt of my dress slides up as I cross my legs, giving him an eyeful of my tanned thigh.

"So, this is where clients sit?" His hungry eyes snap up to mine and an expression I can only describe as wolfish crosses his face. "Actually—" he makes his way around the coffee table and sits next to me. "—no one has sat on this yet. You're the first."

The couch is small, and as he sinks into it, my body inadvertently angles toward him. I rest my hand on his thigh. "Please tell me that's the end of the tour?"

He chuckles with a devilish grin and says, "Yes, so about lunch? I was thinking—"

I don't get to hear what he is thinking because I've basically launched myself at him. I pull on his thigh and with my other hand I grab the collar of his shirt, making him meet me in the middle. My lips crash onto his and he lets out a gasp. Immediately his hands go to my waist and pull me across him so I'm now straddling his lap. I sink down onto him and feel all those hard muscles I remembered feeling last time. My palms fly up to his face. Fingers finding his scratchy stubble, gliding farther up into his hair, and I pull enough to tilt his head back from mine. He's breathing hard, making me smile. "Do you still want to talk about lunch?"

His hands move from my waist, one slipping down to my thigh and the other to my back. He yanks me against him, and I gasp, feeling the outline of his arousal right underneath me.

"I don't give a damn about lunch." He moves his hips against me, and I'm caught off guard as he captures my lips again. His hands slowly move to my bottom, cupping me. His fingers move against the thin cotton fabric of my skirt and inch by inch it rises. He finally gets to the hem and stops, pulling back.

He looks at me with disbelief. "What are you wearing?"

I forgot that I was wearing my lace-edged boy shorts underneath. His fingers brush against the pattern and I shiver. "I was hoping I would get to show you at some point."

"Were you planning on seducing me today?"

I toss my head back and laugh. "Not completely, I was just hoping—oh my God" His lips find my collar bone as his fingers keep tracing the outline of my underwear. Every time he gets a little closer to my center I moan.

His lips travel up my neck and he whispers, "There are so many things I want to do right now but I won't."

I let a groan of frustration escape my lips. "Why?" My earlobe is now between his teeth.

"Because the first time we do this," he whispers, "it will be in my bed and I will take my time. It won't be some quickie over my lunch break. It will last all night and well into the morning."

My fingers are digging into his shoulders, eyes closed. His fingers find their way to my center and brush over it lightly, causing me to shiver again. "But since you came all the way down here, I guess I should make it worth your while. Do you want that?"

I'm unable to talk I'm so aroused. I turn my head toward him and nod. His lips connect with mine as two fingers slip inside me.

His mouth stifles my groan as he slowly moves them in and out. It's unbearably slow and I begin to move my hips, already eager for the release. His other hand attempts to hold me still but I won't let it happen. He breaks the kiss with a ragged breath.

"Maddie…" He trails off as I slow down and make eye contact with him. There is a moment where we're both still and something happens, I'm not sure what. It's strange, I feel like in that moment all of our normal walls are down and we're completely bare to each other.

"Fuck it."

His fingers leave me, and a sound of protest escapes my lips as he starts to move us. I'm surprised by how he seems to easily lift me off his lap and quickly lay me down on the couch with him on top of me. Our feet are hanging off the edge of the small leather cushions but neither of us cares. He pulls the skirt of my dress up to my waist and I see his eyes flare with heat as he takes in the lacy undergarments. Then, quick as a flash, his lips are back on mine and his fingers find their way into my center again.

We're both moving fast now, me riding his hand, him giving me what I want. I'm so worked up that it doesn't take long for the pressure to build inside me. My hands entwine in his hair, and he kisses me hard as I try to come as quietly as possible, recognizing that we are still in his workplace. My body tenses up, my sound of pleasure muffled by his mouth. Then slowly we both relax into the cushions as our kisses change from hard to feather light.

He rests his forehead against mine as we both attempt to slow down our breathing to a normal pace. He begins to slowly move off me and grabs my hand, pulling me up to a seated position along with him. There is a sheen of sweat across his forehead, his hair is a sexy mess and his green-flecked eyes haven't left mine. I can only imagine what I must look like right now, and I can start to feel the embarrassment creep into my lust-addled mind. I look down and adjust my dress so as not to look indecent and look back up at him. He hasn't made a move to fix his now untucked and wrinkled shirt. The only thing that has changed is a grin has graced his beautiful lips. Unable to stop it, I mirror him and actually start to giggle, causing him to laugh as well.

I lean against the back of the couch and sigh. "I swear all I wanted was to get lunch." He leans close and places a quick, chaste kiss on my lips and whispers, "I'm glad we didn't."

He helps me up, assisting me in smoothing down my skirt. The butterflies in my stomach are back and fluttering as his hands move down my backside. I twirl around to face him and reach up to smooth his hair down into some semblance of tame.

He smiles. "There is no saving the hairstyle now,

don't even try."

I avert my eyes in embarrassment and say, "Well um...that was fun." He laughs at my awkwardness. "Come on, I'll walk you down to the sandwich place in the lobby. I think I can still fit in a quick bite."

I'm happy we don't run into anyone in the hallway, for fear of having to look someone in the eye and wonder if they heard me. We make our way down and to the shop, he pays for my turkey club and coke, and we find a small table for two in a far corner.

"What's on the schedule for the rest of the day?"

"Go home. Maybe read on my porch, suntan, relax."

We've worked up an appetite and devour our food in minutes and it's only when we're gathering our trash that he speaks again.

"When am I seeing you again?"

My heart beats faster. He didn't say "can I" he said "when." I know with this intense connection we have I should not be surprised but part of me is. It is nice having certainty in something and I like that us seeing each other is a certain thing.

"Whenever you want." At my response his whole face lights up. "Want to come over sometime this week and meet my roommates?"

"Absolutely. I will be there."

We walk out into the lobby and stop, facing each other. I step forward and capture his lips with mine. This time it's different. Not something that'll ignite the passion of before but something more intimate, more familiar. His hand slides down to mine and our fingers interlock.

Walking out the door into the sunshine, my fingers tingle, and I wish his hand was still in mine.

Chapter Seven

When I get home later that day, I tell Sarah and Steph exactly what happened in Jack's office. By the end of the story, Steph is fanning herself and Sarah swears she is going to try this with her boyfriend one day. I'm on cloud nine for the rest of the day and it continues into the night when Jack texts me asking if I'm free tomorrow.

After confirming that my friends have no plans, we decide on meeting at a bar in Logan Square for drinks and appetizers. For the rest of the night the girls tease me about how they are going to grill him and make sure he is a good guy. When we all start to get ready for bed, the buzzer to our front door sounds.

I call out, "Anyone's boyfriend spending the night tonight?" I see both my roommate's heads poke out of their rooms and shake no.

I press the "talk" button. "Who is it?"

"It's Matt."

I look back at the girls, who are still leaning out of their doorways, eyes wide in surprise. Sarah immediately runs to me and pushes the button to respond. "Hi, we actually have a rule, no jerks allowed after hours…or actually before hours. Thanks."

After she releases the button, I smack her arm. "You know I still have to see him sometimes, right?"

His voice crackles through the intercom. "Hi, Sarah.

This is about paychecks, so I do actually need to come up."

Without thinking I press the "door" button and receive a slap to my arm. "What was that for?" Sarah, her face masked in anger, asked, "He has to talk to you about checks at eleven at night? This couldn't wait for business hours?"

I start to feel queasy at her logic. She is right, what have I done?

Pretty soon Matt is knocking on my door. I take a deep breath and open it. He's standing before me wearing khaki shorts, a tight gray T-shirt and gym shoes that have definitely seen better days. He looks at me and smiles. "Maddie, long time no see."

I step aside to let him in and see that Sarah is still behind me, standing with her arms crossed over her chest. "Matt, we all have to get up rather early tomorrow so please make this quick." She looks at me and I give her a nod, letting her know I'll be fine on my own. She turns on her heel and marches back to her bedroom.

I look back at Matt as he shoves his hands in his back pockets, looking around the room. "It's been a while since I've been here. I see Sarah is as charming as ever."

With a sigh, I close the door. "What do you want, Matt?"

He turns and slowly walks toward the living room, then abruptly stops. He glances down at his shoes and quickly removes them, kicking them off into the corner by the door. The oddly polite gesture confuses me until I see that they are caked in mud and some sort of yellow paint. He looks up apologetically. "Street painting."

He continues on into the front room of my apartment. Usually, I would deter someone from going there as it is currently a mess. My jewelry is scattered across the coffee table, various plates and cups that we were all too lazy to pick up litter the side tables and all the blankets are balled up on the couch. However, since this is Matt the jerk, I figure he does not deserve to be in a cleaned-up space.

He sits on the couch and looks up at me. "I wanted to apologize for the other night when I ran into you on your date. It took me by surprise, seeing you with someone else."

This is the last thing I thought he would say. I remain standing, wanting to keep distance between us. "Um, thanks but what is it you need to tell me about checks?"

He leans forward, resting his elbows on his knees. "I also wanted to say something. I've been going through a lot," —at this I roll my eyes, but he continues on— "and I have been reevaluating things." He takes a deep breath. "I wanted to ask if you would give me another chance."

I'm sure my eyes are practically bulging out of my head. I grip the back of the chair I'm standing behind to steady myself. "Matt what…I don't even know what to say to that."

He gives me a sincere look and the old, familiar feeling of sympathy creeps back into my heart. I was always so quick to forgive him for anything and he knows that. I swallow and shake my head. "I'm sorry but you can't just barge in here and ask that. Too much has happened between us, too much history. On top of that, I'm dating a good guy who treats me well, unlike you."

He puts his head in his hands. "I know, but I'm in a more stable place now. I don't have to worry about buying you dinner or drinks anymore…"

I turn my back on the room to give him a moment to compose himself. This has to be one of the most unbelievable things he has ever done and the more I ruminate on it, the angrier I get. I hear him stand and walk over to me. Turning, I realize he's a lot closer than I expected him to be. He reaches out and puts his hand on my arm. I'm enveloped in his minty scent, and look into his puppy dog eyes.

"I think you should go."

His fingers rub my arm for a moment before they drop. "I will. I guess I just had to know, had to try."

I move to open the door but quick as a flash, Matt dips his head to mine and plants a kiss on my lips. I'm caught off guard and freeze, my eyes wide open, focusing on his closed lids. He attempts to deepen the kiss and that is when I snap out of it. With force, I push his chest and he stumbles back.

I wipe my mouth with the back of my hand. Any pity I had for him is now gone. My whole body is shaking in anger. "What the hell do you think you're doing?"

He doesn't look ashamed, now smiling at me. He probably thinks he's being romantic and all I can think is how I wish I'd kneed him in the groin instead of pushing him away. "Had to take my shot, right?"

I shake my head. "You're disgusting and I want you out of my house right now."

Without another word, he slips through the door which I slam and lock immediately but not before I catch him looking back at me with a shit-eating grin. I turn and see my roommates peeking their heads out of their rooms, shocked expressions on their faces.

I take a steadying breath and say, "I'm okay."

They both begin to rush toward me but I hold my

hand out to stop them. "Before you say anything I need to go rinse my mouth out." They grin and visually relax as I hurry into the bathroom. I manage to lock the door and sit on the toilet before I begin to feel the nausea rise. The sympathy I had for this man is now gone and it feels strange. It is strange to go from loving someone, to pining for them, to making excuses for them, to…nothing.

Jack's face enters my mind and I start to feel better. I remember the way he made me feel today, how his scruff felt against my neck, the fire in his eyes. I let out a huff and pick up mouth wash. If Jack isn't here to physically erase the feeling of Matt's lips from mine, memories and mouth wash will have to do.

Sarah and Steph are waiting at the door as I open it. "What a creep. He is never allowed to step foot in here again. That was assault!"

Sarah goes on and on getting louder and more violent with each threat, pacing back and forth in the small hallway. Steph, meanwhile, gently places her hand on my arm rubbing it in a comfortable way. "Are you okay? Do you need anything? Want me to call Jeff to come over in case he comes back or something?"

I can't help but chuckle at the contrast of these two in their reactions. It's like having an angel and a devil on my shoulder, both voicing opinions that are running through my head at the same time. "I'm fine. I just kind of wish I slapped him or kneed him or something."

Sarah stops pacing and turns to me. "I would say 'you'll get him next time' but let's hope there isn't a chance for a next time." Steph nods vehemently in agreement.

After a round of hugs and another assurance from

me that I'm all right, I head to bed for the night trying to forget about what just happened and focus on the new man in my life I get to see tomorrow.

Chapter Eight

I wake up grumpy. The memory of Matt's late-night visit put me in a weird head space. I check my phone and see that he texted me sometime after he left. Without reading it, I delete it.

I hear my phone chime two more times and upon seeing his name again, do the same thing. I am so annoyed. He sees that I'm now happy with someone new so he decides he wants to try and start things up again.

After spending most of the morning in bed, being a bum, I feel restless. I begin to clean every nearby surface as my mind drifts to my plans for tonight. I know the girls were teasing yesterday about being hard on Jack, but I can't stamp down the bundle of nerves that has taken up residence in my tummy at the thought of him meeting them. It's important to me that they like him and that they don't think of him as Matt 2.0.

Steph finishes work early and comes home to sit on my bed as we go through each item in my closet, deciding what I should wear tonight. "This is the first time you'll see him since being intimate. Let's knock his socks off."

We decide on a light blue cropped tank top and high rise black skinny jeans with sandals. I put on my silver bangles and complete the look with some dangle earrings. Time seems to go slow as I wait for the appropriate hour for all of us to head to the bar. Mark and

Jeff arrive at our place and we all sit on the patio having a pre-drink as I constantly check my phone. Finally, after watching me fidget for too long, the girls decide it is okay if we get to the bar early, and I shoot up from my seat, leading the way to the door.

We all pile into our ride as I text Jack, telling him we'll be there early. He responds quickly and I relay to the rest of the group that unlike us, he will be arriving on time and not early.

"Maddie, maybe that's a good thing, you could use a drink before he arrives," Sarah says, smirking. "I feel like you're bouncing off the car doors right now."

I take the critique and force myself to stop moving.

Once we're inside the already busy bar, we grab a few stools around the bar, deciding to wait for a table to open up. Jeff is telling a story and Mark, Sarah, and Steph are all listening while I zone out, looking at my surroundings while simultaneously keeping an eye on the door. I don't know why I've worked myself up so much but maybe it's a sign that I really like Jack. I sigh and give the bartender a smile as he delivers my incredibly full vodka soda. I try to lift it to my lips and end up spilling some, splashing all over the small purse belonging to the woman next to me.

"Oh God, I'm so sorry, let me grab some napkins."

The woman smiles, pushing her fluffy bangs out of her eyes. "Oh, don't worry about it, fake leather is easy to clean off."

She laughs and I let my shoulders relax as I dab at the rest of the liquid. I look back up and smile only to see her looking at me as if she were trying to solve a puzzle. I wait to see if she says anything. When she doesn't, I ask, "Sorry do we know each other?"

The woman shakes her head and laughs at herself. "No, we don't. I'm sorry. I actually just moved back here from Madison." She extends her hand. "I'm Allie."

I smile and take it. "Maddie."

"Sorry for staring I just...I'm not weird, well, no more than any other person. You just kind of remind me of someone but I can't quite place it."

She brushes her dirty blonde locks over her shoulder. This woman is giving serious seventies rock star vibes. She has rings on multiple fingers and many piercings in her ears. She's wearing a long kimono-style top with a small black bandeau underneath and frayed jean shorts. She looks effortlessly cool.

Suddenly her eyes go wide. "Oh, I know what it is." She grabs her purse and pulls out a small deck of cards that look slightly worn. Confused, I look closer as she tears off the rubber band holding them together and begins flipping through the deck. I quickly realize they are not playing cards, but tarot cards.

"I've been looking at this deck a lot. Ever since it basically predicted my friend's happiness, I've had them glued to my side. I love to study them, and the images are so beautiful too—aha! There it is."

She pulls a card from the deck, placing the rest face down and angles it toward me. The image on the card is of a man and a woman, each holding a goblet out as if they are about to say "cheers."

When I don't offer the reaction she expected, Allie explains, "The woman on the Two of Cups looks exactly like you."

I look back down and sure enough I see the resemblance. Same brown hair, tanned skin, brown eyes. "Huh, that's weird. What does the card mean?"

"Cards can be interpreted in a bunch of ways but basically Two of Cups is signifying a strong pair. Two are becoming one. So did you just meet someone?"

My hand freezes as it lifts my drink, I look at her in surprise. "Actually yes. We started seeing each other a few weeks ago."

Allie gives me a full smile. "Wow I'm getting better at this." She bounces in her seat as she puts the card back, absentmindedly shuffling the deck. "Well, I mean the card didn't come out in a reading, but it must mean something that I thought of that the moment I saw you. Not that it's my business but it seems like this is going to be a strong relationship."

The nerves from earlier begin to disappear as I continue sipping from of my drink. "I'm so glad I spilled my drink on you."

She laughs as a card falls from the deck. Her eyebrows knit together as she turns it over and goes quiet as she looks down at the card. I can't quite make out the design at this angle and ask, "What is it?"

She looks at me and back to the card. "If this card fell out while I was talking or thinking about you, it has something to do with you. It's the justice card but it's upside down so the meaning is different…" She trails off and I wave my hand, urging her to continue.

She studies the card thoughtfully. "Listen this doesn't mean it's tied to the other card. This is probably a whole separate thing, but it means dishonesty, unfairness—I think maybe something unfair is about to happen to you and someone is going to lie about it."

Celebratory mood now gone, I stare at the card. That can't be Jack. She just said we were a strong pair, right?

She quickly swipes up the card and places the rubber

band back on the deck, her smile back in place. "Don't freak out. These are just supposed to be fun, give you a different way to think about things."

I nod and take another sip. I can feel the alcohol warming my insides now. "Yeah, true."

Allie shakes her head, her curtain bangs swaying into her eyes. "God, only a week into being back and I'm making people feel bad."

I laugh, plastering a grin on my face. "No, I swear I'm fine."

I proceed to tell her that I'm nervous about Jack meeting my friends tonight and she places her hand on my arm in a reassuring manner. "You already know it's going to go great. I think maybe you're more nervous about your own feelings and how strong they are rather than the feelings of your friends toward him."

Her sincerity and kindness startle me and all I can do is laugh. I look at her for a moment then pull out my phone. "Since you're kind of new, you might not know too many people, give me your number. We should get coffee sometime."

Her whole face lights up and relief fills her voice. "I would love that."

After putting her number in my phone, she checks the time and looks over her shoulder at a couple walking into the bar. "Ah, perfect timing."

A tall man with curled, dark hair and a shorter woman make a beeline for Allie, ending with the woman throwing her arms around her in greeting. "Holly, Luke, I made a new friend."

I laugh, introducing myself and Allie says a quick goodbye as they head to a table in the back of the bar. I turn back to my group of friends who eye me questioningly. "What?" I ask innocently. "I made a new friend."

****

Before walking through the door, Jack stood outside and took a deep breath. Today had been rough, he had to deal with some difficult clients, and ended up losing two negotiations. He really did not like to lose.

He wanted to put that aside and make a good impression for Maddie's friends. He felt secure in his feelings for her and in hers for him, but the opinion of friends was heavy and easily able to tip the scales.

Opening the door, he scanned the room, not taking long to find her. As if she suddenly felt his presence, she looked up and they locked eyes. Jack stopped in his tracks and just stared at Maddie. She was so beautiful. A memory of her, on top of him with her head thrown back in passion, immediately sprang to mind. He felt his pants start to feel tighter and he quickly started moving toward her in hopes of calming down. The sooner tonight was over, the sooner he could be alone with her again.

Her eyes didn't leave his as he reached her and leaned in, giving her a kiss on the cheek. His hand went to the strip of exposed skin on her lower back, and he turned to whisper in her ear, "I missed you."

She pivoted, staring up at him through her lashes and whispered back, "Me too."

They stayed like that, grinning like idiots, until Jack heard a throat clearing. Looking up, they were met with bemused stares from the rest of the group.

Pulling out all the charm, he extended his hand to the ladies first. "I'm Jack. Which one is Steph, and which one is Sarah? Those two are clearly the most important people here."

The group laughed and went around introducing themselves. Jack could tell they already liked him. The group moved from the bar to an open table, and he ordered a round for everyone thinking it wouldn't hurt to try and buy everyone's approval.

Maddie seemed a bit more reserved at first and he could tell she was nervous. Her voice came out normally, but her posture felt too stiff. After an hour he couldn't take it anymore and leaned down to whisper, "Is everything all right? You seem kind of quiet."

She snorted into her drink and leaned into him with a sly grin. "Oh, am I usually yelling?"

He smirked. "There she is."

She flashed him a dazzling smile, but lowered her voice, "No, I'm okay, I think I'm just distracted."

Guilt filled him, thinking he was the cause of it. "I'm sorry I was late, I feel bad."

She cocked her head to the side and quirked her lips. "That's not what's distracting me."

Narrowing his eyes, he tried to quickly rack his brain as to what else he could have done. Coming up blank, he asked, "Can I do anything?"

Leaning in even closer with a new heat in her gaze, she replied, "Yes, you'll need to stop rubbing my back. I'm finding it hard to concentrate on the conversation." Her hair fell over her shoulder, shielding her face from the rest of table as she gave him a knowing look. She glanced down and smirked. "Seems like you're easily distracted, too."

Still grinning, his hand moved away from her back and draped over the back of the chair as he subtly shifted in his seat. "You are something you know that?"

Her giggle gained the attention of the table.

Steph raised one eyebrow. "What is happening over there?"

"Nothing," Maddie answered innocently.

The rest of the night flew by quickly. Maddie soon came out of her shell and his eyes were rarely on anything else but her. He was having so much fun with the group that they didn't even realize what time it had become.

Jack inwardly groaned as he looked at his watch. He thought about how long it would take for him to get home and fall asleep which would probably be a while as he was feeling way too wired. Waking up for work was not going to be fun tomorrow. He looked to his right as Maddie slid out of the booth and stretched, treating him to a glimpse of her bare midriff and felt his blood heat again. It was definitely going to take him a while to fall asleep.

Finally getting up and out of the booth, Jack announced, "I'll walk you guys home and then I'll catch an Uber." A fast succession of emotions played out over Maddie's face that he couldn't quite read before she replied, "Sounds good."

Steph, standing in Jeff's arms, leaned over and said, "You know, we should all have a nightcap out on the patio."

Her glazed eyes sparkled with mischief and Jack decided that he liked her even more now for her not-so-subtle attempt at acting the wing-woman for her friend. He grinned, shaking his head. "There is nothing I want to do more but I do have to get up early tomorrow." Accepting this answer, the group makes their way toward the door, all walking out in pairs.

They continued to chat in a group during the walk.

He slipped his hand into Maddie's and savored the feel of her soft skin. After a brief pause, Sarah spoke up, "God this night was fun. Made up for last night, right?"

Maddie tensed up next to him and shifted her gaze toward the ground.

What was that about?

"Oh, a certain douchebag stopped by our apartment last night." Sarah said, flicking her red hair over her shoulder nonchalantly. Mark chimed in, chuckling with his deep voice. "God, Matt sucked." Sarah stopped her boyfriend in his tracks and planted a big kiss on him.

Jack faltered in his steps but luckily, he and Maddie were in the back of the group and only she noticed. Matt was at her house last night?

He wanted to ask a million questions. What was Matt doing at her apartment? Did he try anything? Anger bubbled as they continued to walk but Maddie slowed down beside him, making them fall even farther behind the group.

"He showed up, unannounced. I thought it was something to do with work," she said in a quiet voice. "I-I didn't ask him to come over. I just want you to know."

He was taken aback to see her eyes wide, seemingly nervous. "Wait, do you think I'm mad at you?"

"No, I just…you got quiet and look upset and I just…I don't know."

He shook his head, squeezing her hand in what he hoped was a comforting way. "I didn't think you would ask him to come over. I'm mad because I want to beat the crap out of that guy." He tried to abate his anger and asked, "What did he want if it wasn't about work?"

She let out a humorless laugh. "After he saw us together, he decided he wanted me back. I actually felt bad for him until he tried to kiss me and then—"

He pulled her to a complete stop. "What?"

She hesitated for a moment but then tried to play it off with a shrug. "I mean I pushed him and told him to get out and he did—"

"Wait—he actually kissed you?" He began walking again at a faster pace than before. "I'm going to kill him."

"Um, no. I handled it. Engaging will only make it worse."

Jack attempted to keep his voice low as the rage inside him simmered. "He touched you when you didn't want him to. He deserves to be hurt."

A small smile was spread across her face and looking into her brown eyes began to bring a different kind of heat into his system. "Hey," she pulled his hand causing him to come to a stop again. "—I'm okay. If I wasn't, I would say so. I took care of it. But also, is it weird that I like that that is your reaction and...I feel...I'm not sure, touched? You, um..." she started to look sheepish and it reminded him of their first date. "You make me feel safe."

He reached out, tucking a lock of hair behind her ear. He didn't say anything, he didn't trust his voice right then. She admitted something so personal and the way it made him feel was something he couldn't quite describe. He locked eyes with her and smiled.

"I'm glad I make you feel safe but you're right, you can handle pretty much anything. You're a badass."

She grinned as he pulled her forward. "Come on, we've fallen behind."

Chapter Nine

Jack tugged Maddie's hand along until they caught up to the rest of the group, who either had not realized they'd fallen behind, or did not care. The air was different between them, he noticed. She walked closer to him now, held his hand with her right hand and gripped his bicep with her left. He stole glances at her every few moments, feeling his heart lift. Every time she smiled, he felt a tug in his stomach, lust maybe, mixed with something else.

They finally made it to the girls' apartment building, and Jack said his goodbyes to the other four people in the group while Maddie lingered. As they walked up the steps each roommate turned to Maddie as she remained planted to the spot.

"I'll be right up," she assured them.

Shooting the pair knowing smiles, the other two couples disappeared through the door. Before Jack could say anything, Maddie grabbed his hand and led him down the side of the building. He followed her down a narrow, concrete path just wide enough for two people to stand shoulder to shoulder. The only light was cast from the streetlamps placed farther down the road. He could barely see the end of the path where there was a wooden gate which no doubt led to the backyard, but Maddie seemed to know where they were going.

After they came to a halt, she unlocked the gate.

They walked through to the other side, and he turned to wait for her as she closed the wooden gate. Rather than turn and keep walking, Maddie reached out and grabbed his shirt, pushing him into the corner where the gate met the brick wall and kissed him.

Surprised at first, Jack froze momentarily before responding in kind. He gripped the back of her head with one hand and her lower back with the other, pulling her closer toward him. A small moan escaped from their joined lips and he couldn't fully tell who it came from. She fisted his hair and attacked his mouth further; he could taste the alcohol on her tongue. He figured this is what emboldened her, and he was not mad about it.

Finally, she pulled away to look at him. She reached up and gently tucked a loose hair behind his ear. "Sorry, I know you have to get home, but I've been wanting to do that since you arrived tonight."

Her long fingers began to twirl a piece of his hair at the nape of his neck and at her soft touch, he felt his groin twitch. She was still flush against his body so he suspected she felt it too. He made a mental note to keep his hair down and this length forever so as to let her play with it as much as she wanted. Her gaze drifted down to his lips, and he pulled her close again.

She stopped him as their lips barely touched. "I was disappointed when you said you would walk me home and then leave."

Confusion seeped into his lust-hazed mind. "Wh-why?"

She looked up though her lashes and his body twitched again. A slow, seductive smile spread across her face. "Because I didn't want you to go home. I wanted you to come upstairs with me."

She is adorable when she is nervous but this other version of her, bold and sexy was something Jack could be around forever. It took all his willpower to not make a move, curious to see what else she would tell him. "What would we have done if I came upstairs?"

"Well—" her eyes didn't leave his as her hands started to move over his chest, "—we would have indulged my roommates and had one last drink out on the balcony." Her hands caressed slowly, inch by inch down his torso. "Then I would have taken you to my room and given you a tour." On the last word, her eyebrow raised as her hands landed on the waistband of his jeans.

"What would the tour consist of?" Jack managed to stutter out.

"Well, there is my desk, it's about waist height," — she undid the top button on his pants— "and my closet which is large enough that you can go in," —she slid the zipper down — "and then the bed."

Her hand gently wrapped around his length, and he heard a sharp intake of breath, recognizing it as his own. Jack quickly looked around and saw that they were blocked from any windows from neighboring apartments. His attention flew back to Maddie as she lifted up her chin. "Don't worry, I made sure we're alone."

She freed his sex from his pants and her eyes slightly widened, making him twitch again. He looked down and was riveted watching her elegant fingers wrapped around him, this was what he'd been dreaming of since he first saw her. She began to stroke in painstakingly slow movements, he ground his teeth, reveling in the wonderful torture. He caught her eye and was able to make out a slight blush appear over her cheeks. It deepened as he continued watching her. She gave him a wry grin and he could not stand another moment without her lips on his.

His hand flew up around the back of her neck, crashing his mouth onto hers. Her movements quickened, her hand gripping him tighter as they devoured each other. The tension that was building all night would come to an end sooner rather than later, but Jack tried to stave it off as long as possible, he didn't want this to stop.

One moment she was biting his lip, the next she was gone. Maddie dropped to her knees and before he could say anything, she took him into her mouth. Jack squeezed his eyes closed and threw his head back at the sensation, smacking the back of his head against the brick wall.

"Shit, Maddie," he moaned, trying to stay as quiet as possible. His fingers fisted into her hair as his hips began to move against her. She continued to use her hand along with her tongue to tease him. Watching her lips wrap around him was enough to bring him to the edge. Her hand continued its movements, and her tongue flicked the tip.

Breathing hard, it only took a few more strokes before he needed to warn her of his finishing. Lips still wrapped around him, she looked up and took in his whole length. That was the final push he needed, and his body jerked hard and fast at the release. She licked every last drop and Jack wanted nothing more than to remember this visual forever. Feeling like he was glued to the wall, he was exhausted but happy. He tucked himself in and zipped up his pants as she rose to her feet, her eyes looked everywhere but at him. Clearly feeling shy now, he thought she was so adorable that he wanted to laugh.

She began to say something, but Jack cut her off, pulling her into a hug and wrapping his arms around her. Her head fit right under his chin, and he rested his head on top of hers, holding her there. He felt her arms snake around his waist, and they stood holding each other.

"That was…" He tried to finish the sentence but trailed off. How could he describe what he was feeling? How could he say it without sounding too mushy and scaring her off?

A muffled voice broke the silence. "So that was part of the tour." He released her from the bear hug and snorted out a laugh. Straightening up, he noticed the shyness was gone, leaving her smiling up at him. He cupped her face, touching his forehead to hers.

"I really like you," she whispered.

His heart soared. "I really like you, too." He planted a soft kiss on her lips. "I hate that I'm going to say this, but I should get going—" Disappointment flashed across Maddie's face before he added, "—because if I don't, I'm going to lay you down right here and take advantage of you, and I can't do that because I promised the first time would be in my bed. I keep my promises."

She rolled her warm, brown eyes but there was no denying the arousal in them. He grinned, smoothing her hair down in the back.

They walked, hand in hand, back to the front of the building and sat on the stone steps as they waited for his rideshare service to arrive. They didn't speak, just sitting in companionable silence as she rested her head on his shoulder

When the car pulled up, he made sure Maddie got into her building before he left. Sitting in the car, Jack tried to think back to the exact moment it was when he fell for this girl. He smiled and leaned back, reeling in this new feeling that he never wanted to go away.

Chapter Ten

The next morning as I wake up, my eyes go wide with the memory of what happened last night. *Did I really take Jack into my backyard and go down on him?*

There is a moment of panic, but it quickly disappears as I remember the way he reacted to my touch and his promise of what would happen the next time. I loved how we just sat there together on my stoop. I mean, I loved every other part of the night too, but the fact that we can sit in silence, and I can be happy means something. I've only known Jack for a little less than a month and I already feel…how exactly do I feel?

Panic creeps back into my mind. I have only known him for less than a month and I already feel like—gosh, like I love him? This can't be.

I swing my legs out of bed and instinctively reach for my phone. I have a text from Jack.

—I think last night was one of the best nights I've had in a long time. I really like your friends and I hope they like me too. You're worth being late to work for—

My cheeks heat as I read the message two more times. There is a slight twinge of guilt at making him late for work this morning, but he said it was worth it. I'm worth it.

It's a Wednesday and I have my walking appointments at Jack's building today. I come out of my room to see Sarah stationed at the dining room table, cup of coffee in hand and laptop open in front of her. A devilish grin pops onto her face. "Well good morning, sunshine."

I yawn and stretch. "What are you doing home?"

"Mark and I felt hungover, so I opted to work from home today and he's still asleep in the bedroom, Plus, I wanted a debrief about last night from you. I expected you to give him a goodbye kiss and then be right up, but you were down there for an awfully long time…"

My cheeks flush and I narrow my eyes. "Let me get a cup of coffee before I tell you about my dirty deeds."

She sits up straight and takes off her thick-framed glasses, slamming them on the table. "I was just teasing but were there actual dirty deeds? Maddie?"

I chuckle as I walk into the kitchen leaving Sarah calling out for details to be shared immediately. I'm not exactly a prude but when it comes to sharing bedtime activities with my friends, I'm not the one with the spiciest stories. Shortly after the three of us moved in together, it became apparent that Sarah had little to no filter and would share details of the night before that we did not ask for. It proved to be a good way to make us comfortable with each other fast and nowadays it was normal for all of us to be sipping coffee on a Sunday morning and divulging details that might make others blush. Since I stopped seeing Matt, and even before that, I hadn't really had anything worthy of the Sunday morning coffee chat so Sarah's reaction to my cliffhanger of a sentence was warranted.

The smell of the coffee invades my senses as I smile to myself and hear Sarah briskly walk into the kitchen. She leans against the counter and crosses her arms with a look of disbelief on her face. Our kitchen is a decent size with white painted wooden cabinets and a redone white marble countertop. A medium sized island lives in the middle of the room and I move to the opposite end and perch, creating space between us.

Her fingers drum against her arm. "Details. Now. What did he do?"

I smirk as I blow gently on the steaming liquid. "What makes you think *he* did anything?" I'm not sure how it's possible but her eyes go even wider than before, and I put down my coffee before I spill it from the laughter I can't contain anymore. "I brought him to the alleyway right behind the gate and we got…very close."

"Did you have sex in our alleyway?" The disbelief in her voice is lessened by the delight on her face.

"No, oh my God no, but we did kiss. A lot. Then I happened to trip…and fall to my knees and um…caught him in my mouth?"

Sarah's mouth opens in a silent scream as she jumps up and down and I laugh. "This man, I tell you he's getting more and more perfect with every interaction." My head cocks to the side in curiosity. "Why is that?"

"Because he's turning into every woman's dream; a man who will hold your hand and kiss you on the forehead on the front porch but will pull your hair and choke you in the bedroom."

With this, I spit out my first sip of coffee.

My day, after that, is largely uneventful. I complete all my walks and when it came time to walk Charlie I found myself, along with the dog, looking over at Jack's door. Hoping he would come out and surprise us. I can't seem to get that man out of my head.

After our trip around the park, we came up the elevator to a surprise that sent Charlie in a tizzy. Mrs.

Marlow was home early, juggling her bags of groceries and keys.

"Oh my goodness, let me help." I rush over and unlock the door for her as Charlie runs in excited circles at her feet.

"Thank you, sweetie."

Mrs. Marlow is in her sixties and owns her own interior design business. She is incredibly fashionable and always has a smile and a positive vibe coming off her. She had been married three times and once told me that *finding the right fabric swatch was easier than finding the right man* and *when you find the perfect match, you buy as much as you can.*

I'm not quite sure what that actually means but I haven't asked for fear of her thinking me simple. She's pretty much the coolest lady I've ever met. I let her into the apartment and take one of the bags from her arms, following her into the kitchen.

"It was just so nice, and I finished up with some clients early, so I decided to get home and hang out with my favorite man." She says this last part in a baby voice directed at the dog, who sits wagging his tail. I smiled, nodding in agreement.

As she starts to put her things away, I say, "Well, he was a good boy on the walk so you won't need to take him out for a while."

As I turn to leave, she says, "Oh, by the way, I'm thinking about getting more locks on my door. That sweet new neighbor, Jack? He bought me a deadbolt and offered to install it, but I think I'm going to go high-tech and get a number pad or something. So, when I do, I'll let you know the code."

"Oh yeah, that's probably a good idea. Jack and I

were here when Jenny up on twelve got robbed."

She turns, her eyebrow raised. "Oh, you know Jack?" She smiles as I blush and turns back to unloading her groceries. "Good choice, honey, if I was twenty years younger…"

I giggle, say my goodbyes, and let myself out. While waiting for the elevator, I text Jack.

—*Mrs. Marlow is quite the fan of you*—

He responds instantly.

—*Duh. Everyone loves me*—

I laugh and step into the elevator.

—*She, more than others. I believe her exact words were "If I was twenty years younger…"*—

—*Oh no, I've used too much charm. I hope you told her I was spoken for.*—

My heart races as I read these words. We haven't really solidified what we are at this point. I decide now is better than never.

—*I mean I can go back up there right now and tell her that we're…exclusively dating (?)*—

I hold my breath as I send it, suddenly nervous. The three dots pop up and then disappear. This happens twice more, and I know he's typing and deleting. Maybe I should have just said it rather than asked. As I walk through the lobby mentally berating myself, I look toward the front desk. Dan is not there but instead the two men who were with him last week. I pause as it finally dawns on me where I know one of these men from.

"Excuse me, are you a friend of Matt Blumen?"

At the mention of my ex, they both look up and I know the man sitting on the right was one of the guys who stumbled out of The Hutch with Matt the night Jack and I had our first date. He looks a little surprised and hesitates for a moment. Nervously, he looks at his counterpart and back, giving me a quick nod.

"Okay, yeah. I saw you with him one night outside of a bar. Small world, huh?"

He says nothing, still looking nervous. He instead nods quickly and puts his head back down. I find this weird but think maybe he isn't supposed to talk about personal things at work. The man on the left is still staring at me and something in his gaze makes me uncomfortable. I smile at him, but his expression doesn't change. Without another word, I walk out and feel my phone vibrate in my hand.

—*Okay good because that is basically what I've been telling people since I met you*—

I giggle, feeling relief and text back.

—*Well, I didn't realize I was so behind in letting the masses know. Let me buy you dinner tomorrow to make it up to you?* —

We continue chatting for the duration of my day and well into the night and I go to sleep with a huge smile on my face, happy that we're on the same page.

Chapter Eleven

"I told you I was going to pay for dinner tonight." I argue as the waiter comes back holding the bill book with Jack's credit card sticking out of the top.

His eyes sparkle in the low lights, filled with amusement. "I guess I forgot. Just means we'll have to go out again very soon."

"Yeah, and I'm sure you'll try to pull this stunt next time too, and let me tell you, it won't work." I point my finger at him accusingly as I lean over the table.

He chuckles as he finishes signing. Closing the book, he looks at me with his eyebrows raised and reaches across the table grabbing my finger. His fingers, warm and smooth, interlock in mine and gently lay our entwined hands on the table. "Guess we'll have to see."

It takes a moment but then he breaks into a smile and so do I. A silence settles over the table, and my core begins tightening in anticipation. I reach out and sip the last of my wine for something to do rather than send him lusty glances.

He chose a little Italian place close to his apartment and his words from earlier in the week ring in my ears, *in my bed*...Tonight was the night and I felt as though I could not wait, but apparently Jack could.

He suddenly looks down at our hands and begins fiddling with the pen in his other. "Do you want to go somewhere else? Ice cream? Or a bar for another drink?

I want you to pick whatever we do next." His eyes flash up to me and quickly back down. He is so cute when he's nervous.

I reach my other hand across the table and lightly place it on top of his, stopping him from fidgeting. "Well, we could go to your place? Maybe have a drink there? Or maybe…" I trail off and he looks up at me. His gaze is almost hopeful. My voice comes out in a husky whisper, "Maybe you can make good on a promise you made me?"

He doesn't move a muscle except to breathe out. "Are you sure?"

I nod and his demeanor changes from adorable to almost predator-like. His grip turns hard suddenly yanking me to my feet making me throw my head back and laugh. He calms down and we begin the trek back at a normal pace, but the heat never leaves his gaze. Every time we lock eyes I shiver, unable to hide my arousal.

We're stopped in our tracks as we round the corner. Lighting up the street are flashing lights atop police cars parked right in front of Jack's building. Gone is the lust and replaced is a look of concern on Jack's face. His grip tightens on my hand and we both pick up the pace, heading toward the building.

Nearing the entrance, I immediately see Jack's friend Ben—and his face looks grim. When his eyes set on me, I could swear there is a moment of hesitation before he continues forward.

"Don't tell me. Another break-in?" Jack says by way of greeting. Ben nods, his eyes flick down to our entwined hands. "It was on your floor, too."

"It wasn't Jack's apartment, was it?" I blurt out.

Ben shakes his head and looks over his shoulder and

we both follow his gaze.

Mrs. Marlow is clutching Charlie to her chest as she sits on one of the comfy chairs that litter the lobby. The dog must smell us because he begins to whine and tries to break free of his mother's grasp. She looks up and I can see her normally poised exterior cracked and full of anxiety.

I let go of Jack and walk over to her. Kneeling beside her, I place my hand on her arm. "Mrs. Marlow are you okay?"

She looks as if she wants to cry but holds it back. "Oh, Maddie, my home…" She trails off and I stand and comfort her, wanting to cry myself.

****

"What happened? Maddie just saw her yesterday." As his friend's eyebrows knit together, Jack already knew what he was going to say. "Ben, don't start with that—"

"Yes, she did see Marlow yesterday and she conveniently heard the woman talk about getting a new security system for her apartment. What a coincidence that the robbers strike now before she has the new system installed."

"It is a coincidence. A really fucking, weird one but, dude, she didn't do it. Plus, the fact that I've been with her all night gives her a pretty damn good alibi."

Ben crossed his arms and shifted his feet. "These robberies are clearly made by teams of people. She could have told the team. She has been in the apartment many times, knows where the valuables are stashed."

Trying to contain his anger, Jack began to shake. He didn't want to draw Maddie's attention toward their discussion. "Ben," he said in a low, warning tone, "I love you like a brother, but you need to stop right now."

Ben gave Jack a hard look, then turned, waving at another officer. The man came over carrying a bag and handed it off to him. "This was found in the apartment."

Through the plastic Jack saw a small silver bangle. Taking hold of the bag, he looked at it for what felt like forever. He knew what it was. All the air seemed to have been robbed from his lungs. Looking up, he found Maddie still comforting his neighbor. One wrist was adorned with her usual bangles, but they were thin and numerous; he would not have known if one was missing.

Jack cleared his throat. "She was with me all evening, and this could've slipped off or been taken off when she walked the dog. This doesn't prove anything more."

"Jack—" Ben started, then stopped.

"This is not substantial evidence and cannot be used to prove anything." Pushing down his anger, Jack switched into lawyer mode. "She will not say anything to any of the police here and she will provide an alibi of her whereabouts over the last forty-eight hours."

Ben sighed and took the bag back. He paused before turning to leave and said, "I do hope I'm wrong. I just want you to know."

Jack gave him a curt nod, ending the conversation. He glanced back to Maddie, watching as she talked to Mrs. Marlow, absent-mindedly petting Charlie. She was a natural born caretaker. He could see how the older woman was already feeling better just by her presence.

Easily imagining her as a teacher, the kids probably love her with her sweet and welcoming expression and personality that anyone would open up to. Ben's voice suddenly cut through my wonderings in my mind.

People open up to her and she learns things...

He shut down these thoughts, he would not doubt her. He knew her. She would never do something like this. Tentatively, he walked over to the two women. Each gave him a small smile. "Mrs. M, how are you feeling?" He bent down to scratch Charlie's head.

"I'll be okay sweetie. It would take a lot more than this to break me." She tilted her chin up in a defiant look and he saw Maddie smile at the older woman's attitude.

"I don't doubt that. Rather than sit here, do you want to come upstairs with us? I've got tea or alcohol, whichever you prefer."

She nodded and after telling an officer where she would be, the three of them made their way up to his apartment.

Chapter Twelve

This is not how I thought I would be seeing Jack's apartment for the first time. He leads the way off the elevator; Mrs. Marlow and I follow behind, my arm around the older woman. He goes about unlocking the door as my gaze is drawn to the crime scene tape that covers the entrance farther down the hall. By the noises coming from Mrs. Marlow's apartment, the police are still mulling about inside. I catch her doing the same as me—looking at her door—a pained expression on her face.

The officers' downstairs told us they would knock on Jack's door when they were finished in the apartment. "Do you want to go back there tonight, or do you want to maybe call a friend and stay with them instead?" I ask her in a gentle tone.

She gives me a tired smile. "I'm not sure what I could find at this hour for Charlie and me…"

Jack turns. "You can stay here if you like for tonight. I've got a guest room."

She starts to get teary eyed and flustered but nods her head. Jack, slightly embarrassed, turns and walks into the apartment, sensing she does not want to show how emotional she feels. We both follow him inside and I get my first glimpse into the inner sanctum of Jack Delgado's world.

His apartment has the same layout as Mrs. Marlow's

and yet I'm still somehow surprised by how it looks. Walking in, I'm surrounded by the sandalwood scent I associate with him. We walk into the main room. The walls are painted a light gray and the furniture is slightly mismatched in dark tones but it all somehow works. Up on the walls are framed photos of Jack and his friends and family and I long to stand and study them but know now is not the time.

To the left, a large opening leads into the kitchen. Smooth marble countertops are contrasted against cherry wood cabinets and stainless-steel appliances. There is a small bistro table with two chairs against the wall along with a wooden and iron home bar complete with multiple bottles filled with what I assume are various kinds of alcohol along with a slew of different-sized glasses.

This is where Jack heads first, grabbing three rocks glasses. He looks back at us letting the question go unasked.

"Whiskey," Mrs. Marlow says, then walks out, heading for the couch.

I'm left standing there and let out a breath. "Make it two, I guess."

He raises a surprised eyebrow. "You drink whiskey?"

I shrug. "Tonight, I will."

His mouth falls into a straight line, unamused. He bends down and pops back up with a bottle of red wine. He looks back at me and I can't help but smile and nod in approval, my heart fluttering at how he seems to know me so well already. Quickly, he does away with the cork and pours me a glass. He walks over and hands it to me, our fingers touching.

"I just want to let you know this is not how I thought

the night would turn out."

I giggle. "This isn't how I thought I would see your apartment." His grin fades as his fingertips reach out and brush my cheek. My eyes close and I lean my cheek into his palm. "I can't believe this happened"

He whispers, "Me either."

I feel this breath on my cheek, and I want so badly for him to lean in and kiss me but I'm also very aware of the scared woman sitting in the next room. I open my eyes and see he is an inch away, staring at my lips.

"You better pour her drink; we shouldn't keep her waiting."

He sighs and nods, stepping back. I turn and walk into the other room where Mrs. Marlow is standing, staring out the window, Charlie in her arms. At the sound of my steps, she turns and moves toward the couch. "I do hope my tragedy has not upset your and Jack's plans for tonight." She raises a suggestive eyebrow and I let out a real laugh which brings a knowing smile to her face.

Jack enters, a glass in each hand. "What did I miss?"

"Nothing," I say, a little too fast. My cheeks are heating up and a curious look passes his face.

Mrs. Marlow jumps in. "Oh, I was just teasing Maddie. Come, sit."

We all plop down on the couches, Mrs. Marlow and I on one, Jack on the other as Charlie sniffs around our feet. A silence settles as we all take a sip. My mind starts to whirl as I think about the events of tonight. I break the silence and blurt, "Has anything struck either of you as odd around here lately?"

They both swivel their heads toward me with confused looks. I continue on, my mind working faster than my mouth can get the words out. "I mean, something around here had to have changed for this team or whatever to start targeting this building. I noticed there are new people working the front desk but like, people get new jobs all the time so maybe that's not something weird…" I trail off as I see Jacks lips go up in a lop-sided quirk. "What?"

He shrugs, then takes a sip of his drink. "Nothing, I just—that reminded me that you listen to those true crime things."

Mrs. Marlow has already finished her drink and is staring off into the distance. "Now that you mention it, I do feel as if I've noticed a bit more staff turnover. I've lived here a long time, and I feel like it's never been this much this fast. Good thinking, Maddie."

I smile but the gears are still turning, there must be something else that has changed but I just haven't seen it. A knock on the door makes me jump and Charlie growl. Jack is immediately on his feet. Opening the door, he lets his friend Ben step through, and they both stiffen, eyeing each other.

What the hell happened in the last twenty minutes to warrant these reactions?

He looks past Jack to where we're sitting. "Mrs. Marlow, we're done with your apartment. You're free to go back in."

She slowly gets to her feet, showing her real age for the first time all night, and leans down to grab her dog. "Thank you but my handsome young neighbor has graciously offered his second bedroom for the night, and I will be taking him up on the offer. After that I believe I'll be staying in a hotel until a service can come in a scrub the place clean of the intruders."

My lips twitch. I love how dramatic she is.

Ben nods his head and turns to leave, but Mrs. Marlow isn't finished. "You would do well to check the employee records of this building. Maddie here has keenly observed there has been much turnover and it seems suspect."

His attention turns from her to me as I speak up. "It's also weird that most of the robberies have taken place in the daytime. But this one happened at night. It's a lot riskier, more people around. Maybe they're escalating?"

He stares at me hard as if he's trying to piece something together but is knocked out of it by Mrs. Marlow's impatient voice. "Now, officer, I will gladly thank you to walk me to my home while I grab a few things and then you can leave."

I'm finding it very hard to hide my full-on smile now. Mrs. Marlow is my hero; I want to be as cool as her when I grow up.

Ben hesitates for a brief moment, looking as if he wants to give an excuse but numbly nods his head, retreating out into the hall but not before he gives Jack one more knowing look. Mrs. Marlow tells us she'll be right back and leaves.

I turn to him once we're finally alone. "What happened with your friend?"

An uneasy look graces his beautiful face as he rubs his hand over his stubble. "I need to tell you something and I was waiting for a moment alone." He walks over to me, his arms crossed over his chest. "Ben told me that they found something in her apartment that wasn't supposed to be there. A silver bracelet…" He trails off as he looks down at my arm.

Confused, I follow his line of sight and look down at my bracelet-adorned wrist and back to him. "I'm sorry. Do you mean—" I cut myself off and look down again. I spread out the thin bangles across my arm and quickly count. I have five on. I usually have six.

My stomach drops and I look up at Jack, panicked. "Maybe I took it off or something when I was walking Charlie right? I mean, I'm not sure why I would or maybe it fell off? Although they don't fall off so…so I'm not sure—" I begin to pace back and forth.

"Oh my God. It was planted. Someone is framing me but how would they get one of my bracelets? Or maybe someone knows I wear them, and they went out and bought one and I've just left one of mine at home? My God this is unfair—"

I stop talking as something sparks in my memory. The upside-down justice card. That girl Allie said something unfair was going to happen to me. I need to text her and tell her she's eerily talented at tarot. The randomness of this thought starts to make me laugh.

"Maddie."

I stop and realize how crazy I must look. Jack's hands are on my arms, and he is holding me in place. "Maddie, it's okay. I know you didn't have anything to do with this. Ben was telling me because he is a friend, and because he's a good cop. You're going to be fine, I promise."

I shake my head. "This is crazy. Right?"

"Yes, it truly is. But now you have the best lawyer in the city on your side and you are going to be fine."

I snort. "You're the best lawyer in the city?"

His hand flies to his chest, landing over his heart. A pretend look of hurt crossing his face. "Here I am just trying to help you out."

My arms snake around his neck. "I'm sorry, you are,

and thank you for that." I look into his eyes and for a moment, I'm able to forget this bomb he just dropped.

His hands are firmly on my waist, and he becomes serious again. "I'm on your side. I promise."

He pulls me into a hug. My head rests on his shoulder and his fingers stroke my back. The door handle rattles, and Mrs. Marlow walks into the apartment with a small suitcase and a weekender stuffed to the brim. Charlie happily trots behind her.

I lift my head from the safety of Jack's neck and sigh. "I should go."

Jack pulls back and his thumb brushes over my cheek. "Let me order you a rideshare." I nod, too tired to take the bus. Walking over to the older woman, I take the bag off her arm. "Let me help you get settled in the guest room."

We flick the light switch on as we walk into the guest room. It's very simple in decoration. A bed, a desk and a bookshelf are in there, a few boxes are stacked in the corner. On the right is a door that leads to a Jack and Jill-style bathroom that is shared with the master bedroom. Curiosity overcomes me and I mumble something about grabbing fresh towels as I cross the bathroom and take a peek into Jack's bedroom.

Right in the middle of the room is a large, comfy looking bed with a navy comforter. The bed frame, entertainment system and nightstand are all dark wooden pieces; and the walls are decorated with framed posters from various concerts. Across the space is a door that is slightly open. I walk over to it, giving into my nosiness to discover he has a walk-in closet. A handful of suits hang along the right side with a couple of nice sweaters and shirts and on shelves are various shirts and pants folded neatly. I start to panic at how clean Jack seems, no man living alone is this clean, until I look down and see the mountain of shoes and workout clothes all in one large pile. A relieved sigh escapes me as I look on the left side of the closet where the shelves are sparse. Instead of clothing, there are various items; a football, some comic books, a small keepsake box, but one in particular catches my eye.

A framed photo of a younger Jack with his arms around an older woman, she must be his grandmother. She has the same eyes as him, warm with flecks of green. They both look so happy, and I feel a tug at my heart as I wonder if I'll ever meet her. Surprise overtakes me when I realize the thought that popped into my head, and I'm struck again by how deep my feelings are for this man even though we haven't known each other that long. I make my way out of the closet and am greeted with an amused looking Jack.

"Snooping?"

"Um…well yeah, actually, sorry." I feel embarrassed but he laughs. "That's all right. I don't really have much for you to look at. Plus, all the real juicy stuff is obviously in a safety deposit box in a completely different city. I don't want to make it too easy for you." I smile as he slides his hand into mine, the warmth filling me up after a somewhat hectic night. "The car is almost here."

I nod and lean in to plant a sweet kiss on his lips. Before he can keep it going, I pull away and look into his green flecked eyes. "I'll head down. You should stay here in case Mrs. Marlow needs anything."

He nods and gathers me into a hug. His mouth settles next to my ear, and he whispers, "I wish tonight had ended differently. I wish you were the one staying over."

I smile and give in to the urge to snuggle my face into the crook of his neck. After a moment I quickly pull back and brush my fingers over his stubble-covered cheek. "Next time."

I give a squeeze and a quick good-bye to Mrs. Marlow and reluctantly remove myself from Jack's presence, closing the door behind me as I step into the hallway. A thin strip of yellow crime scene tape is still draped over the door to the Marlow apartment and my mind flashes back the last time I was in there. Did I somehow remove just one bracelet for some reason and place it down?

I know I didn't but how else did it get there?

I stay still and let the silence surround me as curiosity gets the better of me. The police are gone for the night and the door isn't locked. If I don't touch anything, it probably wouldn't hurt to go in and look around.

I tiptoe to the door, not wanting any of the nearest neighbors alerted to what I'm doing, and gently push the door open. Ducking underneath the tape, I lightly step into the apartment and take in the scene before me.

The mirror to the left of the front door is completely smashed with shards littering the ground, reflecting my shocked expression back up at me. Every door to the cabinets in the kitchen to my right are open, the contents inside askew or broken.

Being careful to not step on the broken glass, I walk farther into the condo. Pillows are torn, their feathers scattered everywhere. Books were pulled off the shelves and sections of shelves are empty, their belongings long gone. The mid-sized television is still intact but is off center. My eyes follow the cord only to find it snipped. "This is so unnecessary."

I walk to the closest open door. It's Mrs. Marlow's bedroom. Using my elbow, I push the door open further and peer in. The bed is upended, the belongings on the side tables are now scattered or thrown to the ground. Part of me wants to explore further; another part thinks this might cross the line. Robbers and police already invaded her personal space; she doesn't need to add another name to the list. I begin to turn when a smudge on the ground near the door to the attached bathroom catches my eye.

Taking careful steps, I move toward the offending mark and bend down. It's not a normal scuff on the hardwood floor. It's bright…it's yellow. It's not raised; it's not circular. It is almost a streak. Someone definitely stepped in something, then stepped here.

Why does this feel familiar?

A chill runs up my spine and I quickly retreat from the room. I need to get out of here, finally remembering the car awaiting me downstairs. Retracing my steps and being careful not to disturb anything, I make my way out of the apartment and to the elevator where I push the button a little harder than necessary.

When the doors finally open and I step in, I feel myself relax a bit more. Putting distance between me and the crime scene erases the tension from my body but not my mind.

Finding the car Jack ordered, I hop in and begin my journey home, the whole time wondering how much of a coincidence it is that Matt's shoes bore a similar color to that of the scuff on Mrs. Marlow's floor…

Chapter Thirteen

"So…so yeah…that's what happened last night."

I let my head fall into my hands. My hair falls down, cocooning my face and the cup of coffee sitting in front of me. Silence fills the room and I sneak a peek between strands of hair at my friends.

Both Sarah and Steph are sitting across the six-person table from me, wide-eyed and slack-jawed. I wait patiently, taking a sip of my coffee, while they process the insane story I've just told them. We're all knocked out of the anxious silence by Mark who calls from the kitchen, "Does everyone want bacon?"

This snaps Sarah out of it. She yells back, "The answer is always yes, Mark. And I love you, but your timing is terrible."

I hear his distant chuckle as he goes back to clinking pans and plates as the aroma of breakfast food begins to waft into the dining room.

Stephanie places her hands on the table as if to steady herself while looking at a spot on the table. Her face is tight with concentration. "So, you think that when Matt was here and practically assaulted you, he stole one of your bracelets that happened to be sitting on the coffee table… and planted it in Jack's neighbor's apartment which… he and his friends robbed in order to frame you…do I have that correct?"

I shrink down into my seat. "When you say it like

that, I sound crazy".

She shakes her head. "I mean yes, but I don't think you're crazy. When you lay out all your recent interactions with him and the fact that he does have access to all these buildings and the whole yellow paint on the shoe thing...it's not entirely unbelievable."

I look at Sarah who's staring at me with an almost pitying look. "For once," she says, "I feel like I do not have an answer to this problem. I want to say go to the police but like...you have, and they think it's you—"

"Technically, Ben Martinez thinks it's me. That doesn't mean the whole group of them does."

"—and my other idea," she added, "—is for you to leave town for a while so when another robbery happens and you're not here they can see that you had nothing to do with it—"

I countered with "—but if it's a team they can still suspect me of helping plan it or something."

Sarah slumps down in her seat. "Right."

A heavier silence falls over the group of us until Mark walks in with three plates filled with food balanced on his arm and sets them down in front of us. Straightening again, he takes a look at all of us and simply says, "I'll...uh make more coffee."

I throw him a grateful smile as he walks away and look back at my two best friends. "If you guys think this is kind of...I don't know, scary or too much, I have no problem staying somewhere else for a while until this all gets figured out."

"No."

"Absolutely not."

They both answer at the same time with such ferocity it causes me to jolt, banging my elbow on the wooden surface. Sarah reaches across the table and grasps my hand tightly. "You are not going anywhere. We're here with you no matter what happens."

Steph gets up and comes around the table, stopping behind my chair and throwing her arms around my shoulders, her cheek rests against the top of my head. "We'll help you figure this out. We may not be high-powered lawyers like your new boyfriend, but we'll do whatever we can to help prove that Matt is up to no good."

I feel my eyes well up as I grip Sarah's hand back just as tightly and lift my other hand to hold onto Steph's arms which are still wrapped around me. My voice cracks as I whisper, "Thanks, you guys."

We stay like that, comforting each other until we hear a confused voice call from the kitchen, "Can I come in now?"

We all burst out into laughter as Sarah yells, "You're lucky I love you, you dummy."

****

"I hope you slept well," Jack said to his neighbor as she walked out of his guest room. He already called the office and told them he would be in later this morning. He did not want Mrs. Marlow to wake up in the apartment alone, not after last night.

"I did. Thank you, Jack."

She was dressed in a smart skirt suit with her hair expertly pinned back. Charlie, already on a leash, trotted next to her and wagged his tail upon spotting him. Jack poured her a cup of coffee, and she slid into a seat at his two-person table with her mug. Sitting opposite her, he leaned down to scratch the dog behind the ears. "How are you feeling today?"

She sighed. "Like I said last night, it will take a lot more than a robbery to break me."

He continued to look at her. "I don't doubt that but it's also okay to be freaked out."

She let out a huff that could almost be a laugh. "Thank you, my dear. You're a very kind man." Taking a sip of her coffee, she narrowed her eyes at him. "You know, Maddie is a very special woman."

He smiled. "I think so, too."

Her lips turned up into a wry grin. "I think you two make a good match. Just don't mess it up." Now it was Jack's turn to laugh as she finished her cup, stood, and placed it into the sink. "I'll be on my way, and I'll be checking into a hotel for the next few days."

He rose from his seat, shoving his hands into his back pockets. Turning around, there was something in her gaze that made him stand up straighter. "Please be on alert, not just for you. The way she was talking last night, I'm sure Maddie will go looking for trouble."

He nodded and the older woman took her leave. Going over to his window, he looked out as he thought about…well everything. How could Maddie's bracelet be at the crime scene yesterday? He knew she couldn't be involved and felt even more justified in that thought because Mrs. Marlow didn't believe it either. His mind kept going back to what she said last night.

Someone is framing me.

Someone knew that Maddie has a set schedule in this building, making her an easy target. Checking his watch, he had time to go down and talk to the lobby attendants before work.

There was no trace of last night's events in the lobby. The crime scene tape was gone, no lingering police presence, not a piece of furniture out of place and it weirded him out. He walked up to the desk to greet the two men stationed there.

"Hey, um, I'm Jack Delgado. I'm up in 806, still kind of new to the building."

The man on the left, who looked to be in his mid-fifties, smiled. "Welcome to the building. My name is Dan." He gestured to the younger man on his right whose features were set in a grim line. "I'm training Kent here today."

"Hey, I guess I just wanted to start getting to know the faces here," Jack said. "After last night, I guess I want to know who works here and know some faces."

Dan's face turned serious. "Oh yeah, I heard. I don't work nights but that kind of stuff won't be happening here during the day. You have my word."

Jack's focus slid to Kent whose lips twitched for a moment then set back into a grim line. Something about him was familiar but he couldn't put his finger on it. Smiling, he nodded back at Dan. "I don't doubt it. I'll see you around."

As he made his way to the office, he made a mental note to see if anyone else was being trained when he arrived back home later today.

****

Three hours passed and Jack had barely gotten anything done. He grabbed his cell phone and immediately put it down for what felt like the tenth time. He wanted to call Maddie and see how she was doing, but since she had yet to reach out to him, he was not sure she wanted to talk. He also stopped himself from calling Ben, but he doubted he would say anything else pertaining to that case to him. He hated feeling useless.

It was why he became a lawyer; he just wanted to help people and he definitely wanted to be the one to help Maddie right now.

Standing up suddenly, fast enough to make his desk chair roll back and smack the wall resulting in a loud noise and scuff mark, he grabbed the phone and dialed Ben. He felt the need to at least try.

Ben picked up on the second ring. "You know I can't say anything."

Jack huffed out a humorless laugh. "Well hello to you, too." He heard the chatter of voices and phones ringing in the background and figured his friend must be at the station.

"I mean it, Jack, I can't say anything. Anything I could say to you, I said last night okay?"

Walking aimlessly around the office, he ended up at the window and leaned his head against the glass. "Ben, please just let me know if I should be preparing for something. You must know I'll be defending her should anything come down."

There's some shuffling before Ben spoke again, this time with his voice lowered. "Jack, you barely know this woman—"

"I know that I'm crazy about her and that she is innocent, and I will do my job and defend her to the fullest extent of the law."

He snorted. "You've been watching too many legal dramas." Jack could practically hear Ben rolling his eyes. His voice turned to a rough whisper. "Start preparing because it looks like she's going to be questioned. We can place her in a number of other buildings where robberies took place. We've got more on her than you think. Be careful."

With that, Ben hung up and Jack silently thanked whatever power it was that made them into friends all those years ago.

He began to dial Maddie, then stopped. He felt uneasy at the idea of her schedule matching up nicely with the scenes of other robberies, not because he thought she was guilty but because maybe she was right about someone framing her. Maybe someone has been following her, stalking her, and placing blame on her. Switching gears, he clicked a button, and started to text Ben on his cell phone.

—Maybe someone is stalking her and framing her—

He waited and watched as the ellipses came to life, signaling that he was writing back.

—That seems a bit farfetched dude. How did they get her bracelet? I saw her wrist, that's a set, she must've given it to someone—

The uneasy feeling grew but before he could respond, Ben kept typing.

—I know you like her but what if she's using you while she's dating one of the robbers? What if she left her bracelet at his house and he planted it there? —

The unease was replaced with anger as he sarcastically typed back.

—Then I'm still right. Someone is framing her. —

Ben sent back a frown emoji and Jack continued.

—So you're saying she has no interest in me. —

—No, I'm saying that she's guilty—

—That she's fucking someone else and using me to get entrance into the building which she already has? —

He was seething as apologies started to pour in

—No, no, calm down, I'm just playing devil's advocate. Come on man, this is my job. I'm sorry. —

—I mean you can always turn the tables and sleep with her to find out who the robbers are…—

He knew Ben was joking now, trying to make things light, but Jack was too pissed and texted back, knowing Ben would understand it as sarcasm:

—Hey that's a great idea. I'll be the honey pot. I've already got her eating out of my palm, now I'll seal the deal and gather evidence.—

He took deep breaths through his nose to calm himself. He was done talking to him and decided it was time to call Maddie.

She picked up with a breathy "hello" that made Jack's body instantly respond, thinking about how she looked at him the night before.

He took a steadying breath. "Hey." Softening his tone, he asked. "How are you feeling?"

"I-I guess I'm as okay as I can be today. How is Mrs. Marlow?"

"She's fine. I came into work a bit late to make sure she was okay this morning. She'll be staying at a hotel for the next few days I guess."

"Oh good." She fell silent; he listened to her even breathing and closed his eyes. "So, I called Ben and I think we should meet to go over some things."

"What? You need my alibi?"

She tried to sound upbeat, and he wished more than anything he could play along but she needed him to be responsible right now. "Kind of, yeah. Look, I know you didn't do it, but I want to make sure we're prepared when the cops want to officially question you, and they will." She sighed and he continued on, "I'm not trying to freak you out but, this is what I do. Can you let me help you?"

"I know Jack. I—" After a moment, her voice

returned and it sounded smaller, more wounded. "I want you to help me. Please."

Jack's fingers curled into a fist. He hated that she felt scared, that someone made her feel this way. "Okay, do you want to come over to my place tonight? I can compile a list of questions that they might ask you. I'll hound Ben for more info if needed." Her sniffled response stopped his heart. "Maddie, it will be okay."

"I know. I'll come over around seven, okay?"

Her voice still sounded small and shaky. He wished he knew what to say in this moment, but his mind was coming up blank so instead ended the call. "Okay I'll see you then."

Chapter Fourteen

"Chicago Murder Heads, you guys okay?"

RJ's voice flows through my earbuds as I stare out the window of the dirty Chicago bus, heading toward Jack's place for a brainstorming/ "prove I'm innocent" party. His call to me earlier today helped abate my nerves but I'm still feeling anxious about the cops thinking I was involved somehow in this. Getting on the bus, the only thing I could think of was to listen to some story that took place far away, to get my mind off things. Clearly RJ wasn't going to let me do that.

"I've been keeping up with the robberies in your city and boy, do they just keep coming. Every time a new heist pops up in the headlines, my list of questions increases exponentially. How is this team—notice I said team instead of guys, I mean, women can be criminal masterminds too!"

I cringe at her statement as she continues. *"How is the team picking these specific apartments? Have they infiltrated the trust of these condo dwellers, gaining easy access? Is it even the same team each time? Is there a ring of thieves living in the underbelly of Chicago?*

"Okay, okay, I got a little over-dramatic there, but to answer the second to last question, I do think it's the same team. My sources have confirmed there is a calling card of sorts left at each crime scene and it may or may not involve a lot of smashed, reflective glass…"

That came as a surprise. RJ's sources must be actual police officers because that is a detail that should not be widely known. I'm sure Jack and I only know about the broken glass because Ben trusts Jack, and me by proxy, to not blab. Hopefully he doesn't listen to this podcast because I'm sure it would be more fuel to the fire of him suspecting me.

"Also, what is the deal with that? What do they think they are, Batman villains? Can they not stand the sight of themselves? Are they hideous with scars and clown makeup? I would ask if they're okay, but I guess if they were, they wouldn't be robbing people. I was also curious if they were looking for something specific or just grabbing valuables. My wonderful source confirmed that they are just grabbing the goods and getting out which immediately dashed my hopes for some bigger heist plot. I love a well thought out plan and sadly these robbers aren't delivering me the intricate details I crave.

"Jokes aside, the police are having a hell of a time catching them. Watch your backs, guys, and buy new locks for your doors!"

****

I ball up my napkin and toss it onto the plate laying on my lap. "Jack, we've been over this like three times and every time ends the same. We don't know how my bracelet ended up in the Marlow apartment."

When I arrived at his place an hour ago, Jack already had a workstation set up on his coffee table. He had research on the current string of robberies, a list of questions that could be asked, and mountains of legal books and papers that could answer any question I ever had about the possible outcomes of my situation. He had taken the liberty of ordering us pizza and had a glass of wine poured for me. If it wasn't for the worrying thought of me going to jail, it might have passed for a cozy date.

Keeping his eyes glued to the legal pad on his lap, Jack runs his hands through his hair. He hasn't bothered to change out of his work clothes, just rolled up the sleeves of his dress shirt and unbuttoned his collar. He looks disheveled and studious and…sexy. I can imagine him as a law student, looking exactly like this, pouring over a book in a library, studying for a test. I wish I could be more helpful, but I have nothing to offer. So, I do the only thing I can and begin to clean up.

The movement seems to remind him I'm here. He looks up, bleary eyed. "You don't have to do that."

I smirk. "You cook, I clean. That's the rules. Plus, this is making me feel helpful." I walk into the kitchen, discarding the trash and place my palms on the counter. I take advantage of this moment out of his presence and try to sort out my thoughts.

I have had a constant bundle of anxiety and fear living inside me since yesterday after Jack told me my bracelet was found in the apartment. When Ben looked at me with doubt and accusation. I take a deep breath in and roll my shoulders back, realizing they've been hunched up to my ears in tension.

Am I just an easy target? Did I do something to someone, and this is karmic retribution? The only light at the end of the tunnel has been the constant support of Jack. Since the beginning, he has been so certain telling me everything would be okay. His optimism was nice but the fact that he was a lawyer, and on my side, felt very encouraging.

"Maddie?" he calls from the other room, snapping me out of my haze. I grab the open wine bottle and carry it back in where Jack, now standing and rubbing his eyes, is waiting. "Just what I was going to ask you to grab."

Snatching up his empty glass, he crashes onto the couch. I gingerly step over his outstretched legs and sit next to him, filling our glasses. I feel his eyes on me as I sip in silence. Leaning my head against the cushion, I look over and stare into the hazel eyes.

"Penny for your thoughts?" he asks.

I smile wearily. "I just wish I could be more helpful or tell you the one thing that would somehow crack the case and clear me of everything."

His free hand snakes out and gently grabs mine in solidarity. His thumb rubs soothing caresses over the back of my hand. He clears his throat, summoning my eyes back up to his. "You've been so helpful. Things will work out, they always do. I'm sorry if this," he gestures to the coffee table, "—is overwhelming but I want to make sure we're prepared for anything."

"We." I whisper to myself. His gentle caress stops and his eyebrows bunch together.

"We. I was never going to let you do this alone. I know you didn't have anything to do with this."

His phone vibrates on the table, and I look over at it, but he makes no movement. "Ignore it, I'll read it later."

I look back at him. He's still staring at me. "It could be important. Could be a career-making case." I try to joke but it comes out flat but his lips twitch anyways.

"I'm with an incredibly important client right now." He smiles and I roll my eyes, earning a laugh from him. "But seriously," his voice lowers, "—you okay?"

I take a shaky breath and nod, not trusting my voice. He leans over and grabs my glass, placing it along with his on the table and scoots over closing the gap between us. His arms slide around me and pull me into a hug. As I sag into his chest, I realize I needed this, a hug, closeness, warmth. His hand runs up and down my back and I breathe in his cologne. My head angles up, and my face is in the crook of his neck, and I feel his hand still for a moment before it continues.

"We can stop for the night if you're tired. I can call you a car to go home if you want." His voice sounds rougher than usual. I shake my head, my face moving over the sensitive skin of his neck and pull back.

"No, I'm too wired but I think maybe a break would be good because I just…I feel bad."

"I think anyone in your situation would."

"Ben doesn't like me and he's probably told your other friends and…I understand if you want to put this on hold for a while."

I feel him stiffen underneath me. "What do you mean *this*?"

"Us, dating. Look I know how important friends and their opinions are and if this is too hard, I mean, I just don't want you stuck in the middle of something and putting you in a weird position with Ben."

"I don't want to put this on hold for a while. We both know you didn't do anything wrong and Ben doesn't not like you, he's just…a naturally suspicious person." Jack finishes lamely and I chuckle. His eyes bore into me, making me want to squirm under his intensity.

"Do you want to put this on pause?"

"No. Definitely not," I answer quickly. "I just worry about you."

He grins and runs a hand through his hair, making it messier and somehow sexier at the same time. "You're the one in trouble and you're worried about me. You're one of a kind Maddie."

If this was a normal night, a date rather than a work session, now would be the part where he would lean in and kiss me. I hope he is thinking this too, otherwise there is something wrong with me, thinking about his lips on mine at a time like this…

I try to diminish the growing sexual tension that I'm feeling. I look down at my hands. "I never asked, what are your rates? I need to pay you for all this."

He grins, and I look up. "I'm doing this pro-bono so don't worry."

I snort. "Absolutely not."

His smile widens. "It's too late, I've already turned in the paperwork, it's all official." His smugness makes me smile.

His face inches closer to mine and suddenly his features turn serious.

"Maddie?"

"Jack?"

"I want to state that I invited you over tonight to work—"

I nod, my eyes sweeping across his stubbled jaw.

"—and not to take advantage of you in an emotional state—"

I feel myself beginning to close the space between us.

"—but I really want to kiss you right now." He finally finishes his sentence. Our lips are so close together, but he holds back, waiting for me, giving me a chance to shoot him down. His breath tickles my lips.

"I really want you to kiss me, too."

I lock eyes with him and feel mine go wide as I recognize the lust that must be mirrored in my own stare.

His mouth softly brushes over mine once, twice. My breath quickens and I lean my forehead against his. "Jack, kiss me."

Those seemed to be the magic words that unleash him. His hand cups the back of my head, crushing my mouth to his. My fingers find their way up to the hard, stubbled jaw I stared at moments ago and softly slide up until they tangled in his long hair. I pull him toward me and sink back into the couch, dragging him on top of me. He plants his hands on either side of me, holding himself so his weight doesn't slam into me. My palms run over his shoulders and down his hard biceps.

His tongue explores my mouth quickly before he pulls back from me, beginning to plant kisses along my jaw and throat. A sound escapes me that I don't recognize, an almost whimper of delight. I feel him smile against my taut throat and feel his chest rumble as he hums his approval. His hand skims down the side of my ribcage and under my thin T-shirt. The first touch of his warm fingers on my bare stomach causes my breath to hitch in my throat and then they begin their slow, arduous journey up my body, bringing the bottom of my T-shirt along with them.

"Maddie?"

My eyes fly open, I didn't even realize they had drifted shut, and find him staring at me. His breathing is as uneven as mine and his fingers have paused right under the edge of my bra. "Are you…"

He falters, and I can see uncertainty in his eyes, but I know what he's referring to. He's worried that I'm not okay, that I'm mentally not ready for this, that he's taking advantage of me. Knowing all this just makes me want him more. A slow smile spreads across my face and the doubt disappears from his gaze. "Yes" is all I can say before his lips find mine again and his hand fully cups my breast.

Since the moment our lips connected, I've felt heat pool inside me and as his fingers glide along the band of my bra and expertly unhook it, the heat builds faster. He sits back on his heels and tears off his shirt and I pause to watch. Every time we've hugged or touched, I've felt the hardness of his abs underneath the clothes but now, sitting face to face with him I'm speechless. His naturally tanned skin is smooth on the right side of his chest with a smattering of chest hair in the middle but on the left there are a number of tattoos. A goblet like cup is inked over his heart and is tipped to be pouring out water that morph into scales of justice. From there the waterfall of tattoos spreads around his ribcage and continues onto his back, which is blocked from me right now. The artwork is beautiful and somewhat familiar, and I want to look and study each image for as long as possible. The hair on his head brushes the tops of his shoulders and as he kneels before me with a grin on his face, he looks like a romance cover model. "I didn't realize you had tattoos" I sputter out stupidly as his grin widens in amusement.

"I'll let you look at them later."

I finally tear my eyes away from his torso when he moves off the couch and offers me his hand. Confused, I tentatively grab it as he adds, "I need to fulfill my promise." And looks toward his bedroom door.

Goosebumps erupt over my entire body, and I slowly stand and follow him through the door, led by our entwined fingers. He begins walking backward, pulling me toward him until our foreheads rest against each other. He gives me a tender kiss and I feel emotion begin to build in me. I panic, where was the hot passion we had just moments ago? How is this now so… romantic? My brain starts to whirl to life, and I know if I don't stop it now, I'll be too in my head, unable to enjoy this, him.

I place my hands on his naked torso and gently push until he falls onto his bed. As my fingertips skim the hem of my shirt, Jack goes still. His eyes are glued to my hands, and I quickly whip off my shirt, my unhooked bra falling off my arms. I pause to look at him and he swallows hard, his gaze roaming over every inch of me. I smile, enjoying the fact that with one movement, I've made him look like a man about to devour a feast. I undo the button on my jean shorts and let them fall off so I'm standing there in my black cotton underwear. I see his fingers curl into the sheets and his chest starts moving again, he's waiting.

I climb onto his lap and straddle him; his hands holding me in place around my waist. "You are absolutely beautiful" he groans as I push my weight down on him, the warmth of my apex against his bulge. He seems mesmerized by my movements, his focus on the point of friction. I chuckle and he glances up.

"Well, are you just going to stare at me or are you going to do something?" The challenge reignites the blaze in his eyes, and he grips my backside and flips us over so that I now lay underneath him on the bed.

"You want me to do something?" He growls into my ear, biting my lobe. I gasp as his lips trail down my neck, his tongue tracing a sizzling path. Hot breath reaches my chest and I involuntarily arch, pushing my breast into his mouth. He nips and teases me with his swollen lips while his hand is fastened to my other breast, pinching and playing. "Is this 'doing something?'" he growls, continuing the sweet torture. My fingers find his soft hair and I pant as his head begins to move further south, down my body.

"Do you remember that day when I gave you a tour of my office?" I feel the vibrations against my abdomen of his voice with every word he speaks. "Mmhmm," I respond, not able to fully form words anymore.

"Do you remember when I said I wanted to do so many things to you?" His lips softly brush against the waistband of my underwear, and I hold my breath. His teeth bite the band and with his hands, pulls the fabric down and off my body. He pushes himself back up onto his knees and takes me in, completely bare and stretched out on his bed.

Crouching back down, his hands grip my thighs and part them wider as his molten stare trails up my body and locks onto my watchful gaze, a wicked gleam in them. "This was the first thing." His mouth hurriedly covers my already wet center and I cry out.

He licks and sucks on me as I try and fail to not buck against the feel of him. His left hand flies up to my breast, pinching a nipple in between his thumb and forefinger while his right disappears from my view. I feel him a moment later and I grip the sheets between my fingers as he slides two into me. The combination of his mouth and his fingers find a rhythm and it's not long before I cry out his name and he wrings every last bit of energy from me before I feel myself sink back into the mattress.

His hot mouth trails back up my body to my mouth. He pulls away and brushes hair from my forehead and grins. "You ready for the second thing?" I giggle and he smiles.

He rolls off the bed and walks around to his side table and grabs a condom out of the drawer. I roll over onto my stomach and rest my head in my hands and watch. He stops as he catches my eye and I raise my eyebrow. "You're still dressed."

He narrows his gaze and I feel wet heat pool between my legs again. Without breaking eye contact, he begins to unbutton his pants. Slowly he pushes the clothing down and I let my eyes follow. His arousal springs free, followed by an expanse of tanned, muscled thighs, and my core clenches in anticipation while my mouth waters, instantly remembering what he tasted like in the alley. He strokes himself, clearly turned on by my blatant staring.

"If you keep looking at me like that, I won't get to the second thing on my list."

I giggle again and bury my head in the sheets. I hear him rip open the wrapper and then the bed dips under his weight. His fingers softly stroke my back. They move up to my head and his hand grips my hair and lifts my head slightly making me gasp.

"Next time, I'll fuck you like this but this time…" His fingers leave my head and I roll over. He quickly straddles me, our noses touching. "This time I want to see your face when I'm inside you." I lift my legs and wrap them around him, bringing him closer. He brushes against my opening, and I'm pleased to see him take a sharp breath.

"Then stop talking and fuck me."

The fire flames in his eyes again and in one swift motion he enters me, making me moan instantly. He moves in a steady rhythm all the while kissing me. My hands run up his arms and my nails bite into his shoulders. I can feel the pressure building and I don't want it to end.

My hands move to his chest, and I push him, rolling the two of us over so he is beneath me. "Maddie—" His voice is strangled and cuts off as I begin to ride him. His hips buck under me and the two of us move faster and faster in synchronization. His hands pressing down on my hips, making me feel him deeper and deeper. It doesn't take long for me to cry out his name. I collapse forward and his arms wrap around my back as he pumps hard and finishes.

His arms stay securely around me as we both pant, spent. My head is buried in the crook of his neck and I feel his lips press into my sweat slicked hair. I feel like I could stay right here forever and through the post coital haze, the worrying feeling that this could all go away soon begins to fester.

Chapter Fifteen

Using his thumb, Jack made lazy circles over the small of Maddie's back as she lay sprawled across him. He was so exhausted he felt like he would never be able to move again, not that he wanted to right now. After they caught their breath, they ended up using quite a few more condoms from his side table drawer.

He wanted her here, with him, for as long as possible. It felt as if once they came into his bedroom, all the issues they had been dealing with in the real world vanished. He was worried that when they left the safety of the bed, they would come crashing down once again.

"Mmruuph." Maddie's face was pressed into his chest, the vibrations from her voice tickled him.

"What was that? I've sent you to another dimension of pleasure after just one night?"

She snorted out a laugh, making him squirm again. Finally, she moved her face toward him and he felt himself twitch again, but this time in arousal. How did she do this to him? How is it that one look from her and all he wanted was to barricade that door and keep them in this room forever.

"I said what time is it?" She gave him a sleepy smile and he couldn't stop his lips from mirroring hers. He lazily looked over at the clock, reading the time, one o'clock. The tired look didn't leave her face when she rasped out, "So do you want to order me a car or…?"

"Absolutely not." He grabbed her arms and hauled her up, so her head was level with his on the bed. "You will be staying here because while I'm tired now, I'll be calling into work tomorrow so I can continue checking things off of my list."

Even with the shadows coating the room, he could see her blush. He loved that after everything they just did, he could still make her blush.

She leaned in and gave him a quick kiss before getting up. "Well, I mean, if you insist."

"Where are you going?" he whined while internally laughing at himself for sounding so ridiculous. "I'm grabbing my phone from the living room."

He barely heard her as she walked, naked, toward the door. She looked over her shoulder and smirked. Jack called out, "You're lucky I don't have any buildings directly in front of my window. You'd be putting on a show." Coming back into view a moment later, she made a rude gesture and slid into bed. Placing both phones on her side table, she scooted toward him and snuggled in, placing her hand on his chest.

He picked it up and played with her fingers absentmindedly. "One of the first things I noticed about you was your hands."

"That's weird." She whispered back in amusement. Jack brought her hand to his mouth and placed kisses on the pads of her fingers.

"They're elegant, smooth, and I couldn't help but wonder what they would feel like wrapped around my—" He didn't get to finish because she ripped her hand out of his grasp and slapped it over his mouth, laughing.

"Tomorrow. Tell me what you wanted them to do tomorrow." He looked at her and felt a happy warmth all over. She snuggled further into his side and closed her eyes. Jack sighed, happy to oblige and excited about what tomorrow would bring.

****

An unfamiliar sound blasts in my right ear, waking me from a deep sleep. I try to investigate but find I can only move my head because Jack's arm is currently wrapped around my torso. The sheet's been pulled down in the night and his arm is snuggled beneath my exposed breasts. I follow the length of his arm to see him still sleeping next to me. His dark hair is curling around his eyes and his mouth is slightly ajar. He looks so cute that I almost feel bad for needing to wake him, but this sound won't let up.

"Jack." I whisper. No response. "Jaaa-ck" I sing lightly. I wiggle my arm out of the hold and use my freedom to brush the hair out of his eyes which finally earns a reaction.

"Ugh"

"Jack something is loud."

"Ishmy phone. Text. Clickbushons" His words are muffled by the pillow, and he refuses to open his eyes. I lightly laugh and turn toward the table on my side of the bed to find his phone vibrating. Grabbing it, I use his thumb and unlock it to find a plethora of texts.

"Ben is obsessed with you. He keeps texting." I croak.

"Mhm. Anything helpful?"

I scroll back to where his string of texts started and begin skimming.

—*I just want you to be careful man*—

—*I'm pulling her background for you so until then maybe you'll keep it in your pants? Unless you ARE*

planning on sleeping with her to get the information. —
—Jack where are you? Getting the goods? —

I stop scrolling and rub my eyes. I must be reading this wrong or taking it out of context. This is some weird joke. Jack wouldn't do that, not to me. I reread the texts again and decide to scroll further back until I see the last thing Jack wrote.

—I get it. Sleep with her first, worry about wrongdoing later. Leave me alone now. —

My breathing stills as heat spreads from my chest, throughout my body. Not the heat from last night, not one of lust but one full of rage. I should've known that this would end up this way. Maybe I have a type?

Beautiful on the outside but cruel on the inside. I can feel tears form behind my eyes and I blink rapidly to pull them back. I won't cry in front of him. When I begin to shift toward the end of the bed, I hear a noise of protest and feel his fingers tighten in an attempt to pull me back.

"No." I say and pull his hand off me as I scoot out of bed. I forgot that I'm naked and quickly begin to scoop up my clothes and phone.

"Whasyou doing?" he asks sleepily, but I don't respond.

I run into the bathroom and begin to dress, stopping every few seconds because of the nausea that keeps hitting me. He was going to fuck it out of me? This whole thing was a ruse. He didn't believe me, didn't want to help me, he wanted to help his friend.

I yank my shirt into place at look at myself in the mirror, seeing the tears form again. I sniff hard and rub my eyes. I won't do this until I'm gone. Suddenly I hear a knock from the other side of the door, breaking me from my stupor.

"Maddie, are you feeling okay?"

My plan to leave while he was still in bed and never see him again is now ruined. I take a deep breath. Wait why should I just leave quietly? I should yell, I should scream, I shouldn't let him get away with this but I know why I don't want to. I don't want to be right. I don't want to have another man lie to my face, getting what they want, sleeping with me, leading me on, and then finally discarding me. It is going to hurt.

He knocks again. "Maddie, I'm getting nervous. Please say something."

I open the door to find him standing there in briefs, his hair is disheveled, and he is still wiping the sleep from his eyes. He is still the most gorgeous man I've ever seen and now I know the most despicable. "What's going on?" he asks. "Are you okay?"

I brush past him and move into the living room. "I'm fine. I'll be getting out of your hair now that you've done what you needed to do." I walk to the couch and grab my purse, shoving my phone into it and attempt to do a quick sweep to make sure I'm not leaving anything.

"What are you talking about?" He moves closer and I feel the heat from his body. I move to the other side of the couch and look up. He looks worried. Good.

"I'm sorry I couldn't be more helpful but like I said, I had nothing to do with the robberies. Now that you've fucked the information out of me, I'll be on my way."

His back goes straight and eyes wide. "Maddie I… I'm confused. That's not what…last night I told you I didn't want to take advantage…"

His voice trails off and with him looking like a helpless puppy, I almost feel bad. I spy my glasses on the coffee table and snatch them up before popping the bag over my shoulder. "Why don't you ask Ben?"

His eyes go wide then he quickly runs into his room. I take the chance and scurry over to the front door where I slip on my sandals. He rushes out of the room, scrolling through the texts.

"No, it's not what you think. He was...I mean it's not, it's a joke, I was being sarcastic. Sarcasm through text doesn't read well. Maddie, come on you have to believe me."

I turn my back to him and reach for the door but a moment later, he appears next to me, leaning against the door to close it. "Maddie, I'm serious. That is not what last night was. Last night was amazing and I was honest with you and I'm being honest with you now. You can take my phone and look through all the texts, I swear."

I finally look up and his panic turns to hurt as he sees the tears freely falling down my cheeks. He has said all the right things but maybe I've just been hurt too badly in the past to believe him now. I sniffle. "You and Matt are more alike than I thought."

With that, I yank the door open and walk through to the elevator. I hear a lot of hustle and bustle behind his door, and I press the elevator button a few times. I really don't want him to come out here and see me break down even more. Thankfully the elevator opens just as he runs out into the hallway, now clad in sweatpants and still no shirt.

"Maddie please—"

He is cut off as the elevator doors close and I ride down in silence, arms wrapped around myself, not stopping the tears.

Chapter Sixteen

"What a jerk," Sarah spits as she tops off my glass of white wine.

We're all sitting on the patio and over the course of two bottles of wine and no dinner I've told my friends everything that happened. I cried all day long and my eyes show it. My head is pounding but I don't let that stop me from continuing to drink the pain away.

Sarah doesn't appear anywhere near finished. "I mean," she says, "even if it was sarcastic, what a gross joke to make."

Stephanie has been relatively quiet this whole time and I turn to her. "Steph, thoughts?"

While Sarah is the type of girl who wants to shock and awe everyone, Stephanie is the shy girl-next-door type. She sees the good in everyone and gives way too many people a second, and even a third chance. I already know what's going to come out of her mouth.

After a sip of wine she says, "I think while it is kind of a gross joke…I think you should forgive him."

Sarah slams down the now empty bottle on the polyresin table. "What?" She's been matching me drink for drink and we're both pretty much in the wind at this point.

Steph leans forward, places her glass down and looks at me. "I think maybe if you had kept reading it would've been more in context. Look, Maddie, I think this guy is crazy about you, wants to help, and seems to defend you to his cop friend even if it's in a…weird way."

I mull over her words. It definitely takes longer than usual as I try to think through the alcohol induced haze. I know she's right, but that initial anger and fear were still very prevalent inside me. I feel tears begin to well up again and Steph's eyes go wide.

"Oh, honey, I didn't mean to—"

"No, it's not you. I just, I don't want to do this all again."

Sarah places her hand on my knee. "Don't want to do what again?"

I sniffle and remain quiet, but I suspect that Stephanie knows what I'm talking about. I shake my head and wipe my eyes. "Nothing. Let's open another bottle."

"Yes." Sarah stands and runs to grab it.

Giving me a small, sad smile, Stephanie stays put. "We can drink tonight but tomorrow…"

She trails off and I stick out my tongue at her, earning a laugh.

****

My eyes are not focusing at the moment. After Sarah opened the third bottle, the night was lost. We all began to sing loudly, yell about past boyfriends and curse men in general and I vaguely remember demanding another bottle be opened. Now it's midnight and I should be drinking water and going to bed but I'm staring out my bedroom window, thinking. I'm still upset with Jack. He's attempted to call and text all day, but I've ignored each one. I haven't even clicked on the texts because I don't want to give him the satisfaction of knowing I'd seen them. I scroll past his name and see a surprise as Matt has sent me a text.

I click it open.

—*I miss talking to you.* —

My drunk brain believes it's a good idea to text him back.

—*Heyy we had som good talks too—*

The ellipses pops up quickly and he responds.

—*Are you drinking?* —

Oops

—*No—*

—*Well can we grab a coffee or something soon?* —

—*Yeah ok. Tomorrow?* —

—*Yes! Thank you, Maddie.* —

The phone chimes. I see yet another text from Jack and turn it off.

****

Jack ran his hands through his hair and kept channel surfing. It was only yesterday morning that Maddie ran out of his apartment thanks to his stupidity, and he hadn't been able to reach her since. His mind was on a repeat of those few moments when everything changed. He remembered the feeling of her smooth skin under his arm, her sleepy voice complaining about his phone and then her body going still and leaving the bed. How he wished he hadn't asked her to look at the phone, that he hadn't sent those terrible, sarcastic jokes in the first place.

He just remembered the look on her face as she left and how she compared him to that piece of shit ex-boyfriend. His heart broke at the distrust and sadness in her eyes. He needed to get to her, to explain, to make her listen but didn't really know where to start. He could go to her apartment, but he didn't want to scare her or appear too stalker-ish, especially now that he remembered Matt doing the same thing

You and Matt are more alike than I thought.

Fuck.

He could try to contact her roommates, but he never got their numbers.

Part of him wanted to crawl into bed with a six pack and drink his sorrows away but a terrible smell was coming from the kitchen. The garbage was overflowing, and dirty dishes piled in the sink. He needed to clean both, the kitchen and the memories of hurting Maddie.

Rather than load the dishwasher, he opted to clean everything by hand just to have something to occupy himself with. It took a while, but the task did the trick. He didn't think about wanting to drink himself to death for twenty minutes. Gathering up the trash, he took it to the hallway and into the trash room—only to be hit by a worse smell. Bags of trash and garbage covered the floor; the chute was overflowing with more bags. Not wanting to be an asshole, he opted to bring the bag down to the garage just to do something.

After hitting the lower level, he walked through the maze of concrete walls toward the cavernous garage area where the dumpsters lived. Turning a corner, and walking through the closed doors, the tangy smell of copper hit him full force. He stopped in his tracks; he knew that smell.

Looking around, as he walked toward the dumpster, the smell grew stronger. Trash bags piled high in the dumpster and disappeared up into the metal duct. Next to it is an almost empty dumpster. Someone was supposed to have come and switched them out.

Gently he placed the bag in his hand down and cautiously inched closer to the odor. As he moved around the dumpster, a shoe came into view.

The shoe was attached to a leg.

Jack knew he should stop right now and call the police but the need to see who it was became too strong. He quickly stepped closer and a wave of nausea hits him hard.

Dan, the nice older man who worked the reception desk, lay on the floor,

He was on his back, eyes closed, a pool of blood is under his head. Taking a deep breath, Jack calmed himself, told himself to think. *Vitals.*

Dropping to his knees, he reached to feel for a pulse. He felt nothing at the wrist. He then moved to Dan's neck and tried to find it again.

Is that it? A beat?

Freaking out was not what he should be doing at the moment, but his breath came shorter, faster. Pulling back, he fumbled for his phone and called 9-1-1.

Chapter Seventeen

Sweat drips down my back as I fight off nausea while walking to the coffee shop a few blocks away. I don't let myself think about how this is probably a huge mistake as I listen to RJ's soothing voice.

"My wonderful Murder Heads, I've been inspired. I had movie night last night and watched a film in which a cop infiltrates a famous robbery ring. The robbers are also surfers. Their loyalty is to themselves and the sea...can you guess what it was?

"Well, it got me wondering if there were any real-life infiltrations. If there were any FBI agents who went undercover and got too deep and had to shoot their gun into the sky...or maybe just the first part...ok enough movie references.

"The answer is yes. Of course, there are real life instances of the good guys working their way into the good graces of the bad guys, then bringing them down from the inside."

I chuckle as I listen to RJ speak. The facts she spews are enough to hold my attention and keep my mind off my hangover. As I round the corner, I see that Matt is already perched at a table outside the door and quickly yank the headphones out of my ears. I greet him with a smile and hope it doesn't come off as a grimace.

A bleached-blonde waitress brings out an iced coffee I ordered right after I arrived and it's already lessening the pounding in my head. I sit at this sidewalk café just a few blocks from my house, Matt is sitting across from me, smiling.

Why in the hell did I decide to meet him? Is my heart that vulnerable from what Jack did that I would consider crawling back to Matt? I prop my head up with my hand and try not to look as annoyed as I feel.

"I'm so glad we could do this," he says. "Again, I'm sorry for how I acted last time, I'd been drinking. I hope that guy you're seeing doesn't want to kick my ass now."

I subtly check my watch. It's only taken five minutes for him to mention Jack and I try my hardest not to roll my eyes. "I'm sure you're fine."

He just chuckles. "You are so hungover, aren't you?" A humorless laugh escapes my lips and I latch back onto the iced coffee. Matt continues, "Well tell me what else is going on with you and what's his name. Wedding bells yet?"

Without thinking, I blurt, "Considering we're not seeing each other anymore, I'd say no."

Matt's expression switches from easygoing to interest before quickly moving to sympathetic. He reaches across the mesh wire table to place his hand on top of mine. I fight the urge to abruptly yank my hand away, so I slowly inch it away and grimace. I wish I hadn't said that. Based on our recent history, Matt's going to try and sleep with me again.

"Maddie, I'm sorry. Why don't you come out with me and my friends? Just like old times, okay? You can use a night out."

A memory sparks, and I sit up straighter. "Speaking of your friends, I saw one at a building where I have a dog walking assignment. He was at The Hatch when Jack and I ran into you."

Matt's eye twitches so quickly, I almost don't catch it but he quickly masks it by taking a drink. "Oh yeah. Jeff mentioned he saw you. Haven't spoken to him in a while."

I want to dig a bit deeper. "How coincidental that he works in the same building where you schedule walks."

Matt puts down his cup and looks at me. Something in his gaze makes me uncomfortable, like he's sizing me up. He shifts in his chair. "Yeah well, he needed a job. Buildings like that are full of old rich people and want young guys to do everything for them."

I'm not sure why he says this and why there is an undercurrent of venom in his voice. He must mistake my silence as permission to continue. "While they're living in those luxurious apartments, we go and walk their dogs and open their doors because they can't be bothered to lift a finger."

I keep my features neutral but inside my head, the gears are going full steam. I just nod, hoping he'll continue.

"Those people don't even care about their possessions. Before I was a scheduler with Ruffin' It, I actually walked the dogs. This one time, I accidently took something from an apartment."

I raise my eyebrows in surprise, and he nods. "Yeah, the dumb dog knocked a small, crystal clock over and I grabbed it and just put it in my coat pocket because I already had my hands full. I didn't realize I still had it until I was home, and I felt so bad. I came back the next day and told the owner what happened, and you know what? The guy looked at the clock for a while because he didn't even realize it was his! He had so many things that he didn't realize that a clock set in crystal was missing and here I was, trying to walk dogs to make ends meet."

I'm about to defend the man when something stops me. I can hear the voice of Jack's friend, the cop, listing all the places that were robbed. All the places that I just happen to walk dogs at…

…the places where Matt schedules me.

No. This is Matt. I dated the guy for years. He may be an entitled asshole, but he doesn't have it in him to rob apartments. To that point, he doesn't have the strength or smarts to pull something this clever off.

"Matt," I begin, trying to choose my words carefully. "Have you been…doing something more than scheduling to…make ends meet?"

His mouth turns up at the corners into a bitter smile. "Yes."

I keep my face passive while I internally freak out. He's studying me intently, like he's waiting for my reaction.

"Interesting," I say, as if I'm considering things.

His smile widens and he leans back in his chair. "I knew you would get it."

I try to look relaxed as I bend down and grab my bag from where it rests at my foot. Holding up the edge so he cannot see what I'm doing, I hit the record feature on my phone, hoping to get a confession. Needing to show him a reason for holding my purse on my lap, I make a show of grabbing a bottle of hand sanitizer and rubbing it onto my hands before I look back up at him. "How do you, um…choose?"

He angles back toward me and lowers his voice. "I just see where we have walkers and figure out the key situation in the building. Key cards or skeleton keys or whatever. Usually, one of my friends ends up getting a job there so we're in and out in no time."

My legs are starting to cramp from holding my purse in such an awkward position, but I don't move. This is incredible. "Where do you sell the stuff?"

He reaches out to take my hands which are still rubbing in sanitizer, and I freeze. If he moves any closer, he might see into my bag. I lean in, trying to cover the phone with my torso but his eyes stay solely on mine.

"I want to tell you everything," he says, "but I can't. Not here. Can we meet for a drink or maybe a dinner? I have no problem with paying."

I just want to gag. "I just…I have so many questions. This is crazy, Matt."

He brings my hand, still firmly in his, to his mouth and brushes a light kiss on it. "I'll explain everything soon, but for now I can treat you right."

"Matt, when I was still talking to Jack…he told me that the police said that one of my bracelets was found…in the last apartment that was robbed." I watch as his gaze leaves mine and looks down at my wrist that's still adorned with the metal circles. When he looks back up at me, I continue. "Do you know anything about that?"

"Maddie, you agree with me, don't you? This is making things right, making things fair."

"You didn't answer my question."

Momentarily, his grip tightens on my hand and a jolt of fear tears through me. "Maddie…" He trails off and offers me a smile, one that he probably considers endearing and I think is nauseating. I've had enough of this. I slowly pull my hand out of his, and down the rest of my coffee. Gripping my bag closed, I stand. And make myself smile. "I've got to get going, but I would be down to meeting up for a drink sometime."

Matt just sits there, staring at me, then finally nods. I turn on my heel and walk down the street. It takes everything I have to not look back.

After a block, I dig out my cell phone and call the non-emergency number for the police. I am met with a tired sounding female voice.

"Hi. May I please speak to officer Ben…uh…" I trail off when I realize I never got his last name.

The voice on the other end sounds huffy and exasperated. "Ben what?"

"I'm sorry. I don't actually know his last name, but I need to talk to him. Um he's probably around five eight or nine, Hispanic, short hair, always looks grumpy?"

"Martinez, I'll transfer you."

Suddenly, the phone is ringing again and is answered after two chimes. "Martinez."

After one deep breath, I say, "Ben. This is Maddie Conor."

He clears his throat and says, "Yes, hi, Maddie."

I let out the breath. "Look I know you don't like or trust me, but you need to know what I just found out."

While I relay the conversation with Matt, Ben doesn't interrupt. Intermittent scratching of a pencil on paper comes through the phone and that mixed with breathing are the only factors that prove he's still on the line. When I'm done, he takes a moment to react.

"I want to first say that this does not prove anything, but I do agree that it is suspicious. You didn't actually get a confession or anything so…I mean I can't really do much."

My body seems to deflate. "All I ask is that you look into him. Please. I am innocent and although it's clear that you and Jack don't particularly care, I won't stop until you know I'm innocent."

"Wait, Jack? You know he—" His sentence is interrupted by something happening in the background. I can hear another voice muttering to Ben. After a gruff reply, he comes back on the line, talking quickly. "Maddie, I have to go but I'll look into it." Without a goodbye, he hangs up the phone.

I stop walking and look up at the clear blue sky. What was he going to say about Jack? I heave a sigh and keep walking, wondering what my next steps will be.

****

"He's in a medically induced coma," Ben said. "It looks like you probably saved his life, Jack."

The dumpster area swarmed with police technicians taking photos and gathering evidence. Jack nodded and looked down at his phone which still offered no response from Maddie. He tried calling her three times and texted her, asking her to call him back. He debated texting her the situation but felt like telling someone about the attack on Dan was something that should not be done in writing.

Once the authorities arrived, Jack stepped back, letting them do their work while he thought back to his last interaction with Dan and that new guy…Kent? He remembered thinking the guy looked familiar, but he couldn't place him definitely. Concentrate on the details, he told himself. Face…hair…uniform… watch.

The watch. It was big, shiny—and he'd seen it before. Outside a bar.

He was one of the guys outside the bar, flanking that

asshole Matt. And he worked here in Jack's building. Didn't Maddie say something about that?

He flagged Ben down. "The last time I saw Dan, he was working with a new guy whom I know is friends with Maddie's ex, Matt something or other. I saw them together outside a bar. You've got to look into him."

Ben's eyebrows rose. "That is the second time I've heard that name today."

"What do you mean?"

He tucked his hands on the inside of his Kevlar vest and looked uncomfortable. "Maddie mentioned him when she called me."

It took Jack a moment to find actual words. "She called you? Is she okay? She mentioned Matt?"

"Yes to all three questions. I can't get into it but rest assured, I'll look into this Matt guy."

Ben began to turn, but Jack clasped his hand around his bicep, swinging him back around. Lowering his voice, he asked, "How did she sound?"

"She's definitely freaked out, still mad at me and you, but she sounds…determined. Strong."

Jack stuck around for a while longer before finally heading back up to his apartment. Opening his laptop, he immediately googled the dog walking business that Maddie worked for. Scrolling through photos and lists of employees, he found two Matts and a quick social media search led him to the correct one.

He could not help but think Matt looked like a jackass in all his photos. Stupid face with a stupid smile. Photo after photo of him and his look-alike friends blurred past his eyes until he found one with Maddie. She was in a booth at a bar with Matt's arm thrown around her shoulders. He's looking down at her with a smug smile on his face. She looked beautiful as always but he noticed her smile didn't reach her eyes. Actually, Jack felt she looked uncomfortable, not how she looked when she was with him.

He knew he could make her really smile…or at least he did once. Maybe with time, he could have her smile at him again.

Chapter Eighteen

It has been three days since I saw Jack and two days since I figured out Matt was insane. After meeting him—and the call to Ben—I went ahead and cancelled all my walk assignments for the next few days. I just couldn't go to Jack's building and after everything I learned about Matt, the thought of leaving the house felt overwhelming.

Matt texted, asking when I was free for that drink. I gave a non-committal response about maybe having time this weekend. Thankfully, he hasn't followed up.

To their credit, Sarah and Stephanie did not pry too much. We've all known each other long enough to know when to leave the other alone. I've basically stayed in my room, watching terrible reruns on the TV, and attempting to avoid my problems. I've also been thinking about Jack nonstop.

I know my friends are right and that I should answer one of his numerous calls or texts. I miss him and really want to talk to him about all this. I've only known the man a short while, but I've come to realize I trust him. A lot. I want to know his thoughts on the situation, what I should do, and I want him to just make me feel better.

Yet again, my mind wanders to that last night in his bed, how he looked at me, touched me, tasted me. I feel heat pool from my belly into my center and I immediately stop the thoughts and roll out of bed.

Looking at my reflection in my mirror, I cringe. My hair is matted and sticking up on one side. I have dark circles under both eyes and my skin is shiny from going unwashed for too long. Note to self: never become unemployed. If this is how I look after three days of voluntarily doing nothing, I shudder to think what would happen to me in a longer period of time.

After jumping in the shower and taking longer than usual, I feel a bit more normal. Sitting on the end of my bed in a white fluffy robe, I stare down at my dark phone. I need to get over myself and just do it, just call Jack. Be a grown up.

I unblock him from my messages and immediately the small room is filled with chimes as all the messages he's been trying to send me flood my inbox.

—Maddie I'm sorry—

—please let me explain—

—I need to talk to you—

—I feel so dumb, it was just a terrible joke—

It continues on like that. Message after message of apologies and begging to talk. I scroll to the very bottom and feel tears fill my eyes.

—If this is what you want then I'll stop. I just want you to be ok. You deserve the best—

This isn't what I want, not at all. I press "call" and wait as anxiety quickly fills my body. After three rings I get concerned that maybe he doesn't want to talk to me now, maybe I missed my chance. I glance at the clock on my nightstand and realize he's on his commute home from work. Maybe the cell is deep in his bag, and he can't hear it ringing. What if he's staying to work late? What if—

"Maddie?" The relief in his voice blasts from my

phone, knocking me out of my reverie.

"Jack. Hi…I—"

"I'm so sorry. You have to know I didn't mean those things and it was out of context but that doesn't matter anyway because it doesn't make it okay."

"Jack, I know."

"And I have so much to tell you. I think I have a way to clear your name but before I get to that I just need to tell you that after these past days I've just missed you so much. I'll never be able to tell you how sorry I am. I feel like a total ass."

I pull the phone away from my ear as he keeps talking and I can't help but smile. He's so panicked and in full lawyer debate mode and…it's kind of cute.

"Jack!" I yell into my phone. The rambling stops and I continue to smile. "I forgive you. I was just so emotional and read into things and…well I really miss you too, and I know we were only seeing each other for a little while but I need you and your help right now."

His relieved sigh echoes through the other end of the phone. "Of course, and before I start to get all mushy on you, I need to tell you something. Your ex— that Matt guy? Do you remember his friend outside the bar that first night?"

"Yes. He works in your building."

"Yeah, well he was working with Dan, the older guy—."

"Oh I know Dan, he's so nice."

"—he's now in a coma at the hospital, Maddie. I found him knocked out behind the dumpsters."

"Oh my God. He was…are you okay?"

I hear shuffling sounds on the other end before he answers. "Sorry I'm just walking into the building now.

I'm all right. I've had time to calm down but Maddie, it's just too weird that he started working here, then the robberies happened and now there's an attack. The reason I ask about Matt's friend is because the last time I spoke with Dan, this friend was working with him. I would bet on my life that he was involved in it. And not to sound like the jealous boyfriend but I really think Matt might…know something."

My stomach rolls as my denial of Matt being involved melts away, or what little denial was left anyways. "I need to tell you something, too. I had coffee with Matt."

There is a pause on the other end of the phone, then he says, "Oh?"

"Yes, and it was…well, he kind of told me, in not so many words, that he is definitely up to something, I mean, he didn't actually admit to anything though."

I give him a replay of our conversation and how I spoke to Ben afterwards. When I'm finished talking, I can hear his keys jingling, signaling he made it to his apartment door. The echo-like sounds tell me he's put me on speaker phone.

"Have you seen or heard from him since then?"

"Yeah. I kind of told him I'd grab a drink with him, but I've been putting it off. I've basically stayed in my apartment since then but it's not like he doesn't know where I live. If he wanted to see me, he would probably just come over."

I stop short as the memory comes back of Matt sitting down on the couch. In front of the coffee table. Of him trying to kiss me.

"Maddie what's wrong?" Jack's voice comes out worried.

"He didn't deny planting my bracelet. He took my bangle, Jack. It's the only possibility. All my stuff was sitting on the coffee table when he invited himself in. I want to meet up with him again and record our conversation."

"Maddie, I don't want you seeing him again. This is way too dangerous now."

"Jack, I really think I'll be fine, and I really need to do something about this. I'll make sure it's a public place."

"Maddie, please?"

"I'll give you all the information and I'll call you right after."

He sighs and I can imagine him rubbing his eyes in frustration, his dark locks falling over his forehead. I wish I was there to soothe him, to wipe that worried look right off his face. After a pause his voice comes back on, laced with mischief. "What if I come with?"

Chapter Nineteen

I finally responded to Matt and told him I was free for a drink that night. After hemming and hawing, he suggested a bar near the Gold Coast. I wasn't surprised at the choice. Not only was it close to all the buildings that had been targeted but the bars in that area carried a particularly douchey vibe that suited Matt well.

After looking up a few, I suggested we meet at Butch's, a bar with multiple, semi-private areas. After confirming with Matt, I relayed all the information to Jack. It was his idea to sit in another room, positioned so that he could have a line of sight to me. This way, he reasoned, I'd have space to try and get information out of Matt while Jack felt better about me being alone with my ex.

As I dressed for the night, I found myself agonizing over what to wear. Not because I wanted to impress Matt, but because this would be the first time I saw Jack since I walked out of his apartment. With every shirt or dress I tried on, I imagined his heated stare across the bar and a pang of arousal shot through my body. I finally decided on sundress with a tie in the front, exposing my cleavage, with the intent to see that stare I'd been fantasizing about while also distracting Matt enough to let his guard down.

Matt and I decided to meet at seven, so Jack and I planned to get there and in position around six forty-five. The bar is humming with life when I arrive at the prearranged time, busy enough that it takes me a moment to find an open table. The bar is styled as an Irish pub with dark wooden tables and walls littered with various beer signs and black and white photos, quite the contrast to the hip hop music blasting through the speakers.

To the left of the entrance, is a front room; to my right is a long bar. At the end of the bar, another room is visible and presumably beyond that is the kitchen and bathroom. Groups of men and women in suits and business casual clothing are scattered across the room with buckets of beer in front of them. This bar definitely attracts the finance guy crowd. I roll my eyes and scour the front room for a free table, finally finding one in the front corner. I make my way over and realize how perfect the placement is for my mission. I take the seat with the back against the windows and the street outside. This will force Matt to take the one putting his back to the rest of the bar.

Situating myself in the chair, then fanning my dress and tossing my hair over my shoulder, I feel eyes on me. Before I can look up, a waitress comes up to me asking for my order. After sending her off with my order for a cider, I still feel the eyes on me and look up. There is a slim line of vision toward the back room, giving me access to a few tables. Sitting in the exact center I see a man in a tight gray T-shirt and black shorts with a faded baseball cap pulled low with dark hair curling out the bottom.

Jack.

He looks up, tips his hat up and my breath catches in my chest. It's only been a handful of days, but I forgot how beautiful he was. It seems our time apart had the same effect on him as I see his eyes focus on my outfit.

His body posture tenses and the hungry look I've dreamt about sends shivers up my spine. A wetness begins to pool between my legs, and I squirm, willing it to go away before my guest joins me.

This was a bad idea, having him here. I won't be able to focus on the task at hand. He continues looking at me and a slow seductive smile crosses his face. I smile back and shake my head. He looks down at his phone and quickly types something out. Seconds later, text chimes ring out from my purse. I get my phone out and look at the new message.

—God you're even more beautiful than I remember—

Tears prick my eyelids and I quickly blink them away as another message pops up.

—It's taking everything in my power to not come over to you right now—

*—Stop distracting me—*I type back, adding a flush-faced emoji.

I see him smile at my phone and look up at me but at that moment, Matt rounds the corner into the room and sees me. I quickly look over at him and wave, focusing on him and still feeling Jack's eyes on me. Once my ex is near, he pulls me into a hug and as my hands go around him for a quick embrace, I spy Jack scowling at us. I shoot him an apologetic smile and pull away.

"I haven't heard from you in the last few days," Matt says as he sits down.

His eyes wander toward my low neckline, and I inwardly recoil in disgust but try not to let it show on my face. "Yeah, I think I had just a quick summer cold or something. I'm feeling a lot better now."

"Good."

The waitress comes by with my drink and takes Matt's order. I use this as cover to switch my phone app to record and place it, and my purse, on the table. Once we're alone, he reaches out, grabbing my hand in his. "I know I've said it before, but I miss you, Maddie. I'm so happy we got coffee and that we're here now. I knew I could trust you, talk to you about anything."

"Matt," I say, sliding my hand out from under his and placing it on top of the table. "We left a lot of things...unsaid."

His lips settle into a thin line as he sits back in his chair. The silence is prolonged as the server comes back with his drink and he nods at her in thanks. After taking a sip, he leans back over the table. "I'm sorry for taking your bracelet and I'm sorry for putting it there. The moment I did, I regretted it. I was still so mad about us breaking up—"

I interrupt him. "You broke up with me. Remember?"

He has the grace to look guilty. "I know and I regret it. I thought we wanted different things and then I started this whole...new business venture and didn't want to see you get hurt and then I saw you with that guy...I just didn't think you would move on that fast because I haven't. I can't."

It's taking a lot of willpower right now to not roll my eyes at his sorry excuses—or to look over at Jack. I need to get this conversation back on track. "So you started—" I look around for emphasis and lower my voice, "—robbing places and didn't want me to get hurt? But after you see me with someone else, you decide not only to hurt me, but implicate me, too?"

"This was before I spoke to you," he said quickly,

"and knew you would understand why I was doing it. I want to bring you in on this, Maddie. You work so hard; you deserve to live comfortably. I can make that happen."

He leans back in the chair, reaches into his pants pocket and quickly pulls out his closed fist onto the table. Opening his fingers, I see there is a pair of large, diamond stud earrings in his hand. I gasp and scoot back, distancing myself from the sparkling jewelry. I chance a glance up toward Jack and I see him, staring at me, subtly trying to figure out what was placed in front of me. He's gripping the table as if anchoring himself to the spot so as not to come over here.

Looking back at Matt, I see him giving me an expectant look. I remember that I'm recording this and say, "Matt those are diamond earrings. Did you…did you just get those…today?" I ask. He nods and smiles. I put my hands over his and close his fingers over the earrings in his palm. "Matt, I don't know if I can do this."

His other hand sneaks out and grabs my fingers, pulling it toward his face. He rubs his cheek with my hand, and I remind myself not to smack him.

"Maddie, you can do anything, and we can do it together. I'll keep you safe."

Inwardly, I snort at his reply. I slowly work my hand loose from his and quickly down the rest of my drink, using the time to think of what to say. Before I speak though, Matt beats me to it.

"Look I have to go meet my friends to talk over some plans, but I wanted to see you and show you what can come of this. I'll walk you out."

I nod numbly as Matt throws cash down on the table and rises. I discreetly look over at Jack who nods toward the bathroom and gets up, walking out of sight. Matt's hand rests on my lower back but I wiggle away.

"You go ahead," I say. "I'm going to go to the restroom before I catch the bus, but you've given me a lot to think about."

He smiles and before I can stop him, he leans down and plants a kiss on my cheek. He lingers, wanting me to turn my head, giving him access to kiss me on the lips but I can't fathom anything I'd like to do less. When I don't move my head, he clears his throat and straightens up. With a brief smile, I watch him walk out the door before I quickly spin on my heel and power walk to the bathroom.

I turn into a wood-panel-lined hallway littered with doors all bearing "gender neutral" on the front. I cautiously walk down the hallway wondering which door Jack is behind when suddenly the door to my direct left opens and a tanned arm shoots out, pulling me in. I'm disoriented as the hands spin me around and pins me to the now closed door. My eyes adjust to the dim lighting inside the single person bathroom. Jack tears off his baseball cap and I'm only given a few seconds to admire him up close until his hands fist my loose hair and his lips come crashing down on mine.

****

Jack couldn't help himself. The moment he saw Maddie walking by the restrooms, his possessive, caveman genes kicked in and he grabbed her. Sitting at that table and watching while she was with that asshole was torture but then again, maybe it was a good thing he was sitting. The moment he saw what she was wearing, he would've had a hard time walking around because apparently that's all it takes now, just a glimpse of her and he gave hard as wood a whole new meaning.

Now his lips were on hers and it was proving difficult to stop, even harder now that she was gripping the front of his shirt as if she were holding on for dear life. His mind flashed back to that night when she lay on his bed, looking up at him through her thick lashes, the way she felt underneath him, the way her hands had marked his body. He involuntarily thrusted, pinning her to the door using the length of his entire body and he couldn't ignore the whimper that escaped from her. She's missed him just as much as he missed her and he could not believe how stupid his thoughtless texts were. She was incredible, she deserves the world, she…probably doesn't need to be groped in a bathroom.

It's with that thought that he attempted to pull away but Maddie held on tight to his shirt. He began to smile and move his lips from hers, to her jaw and down her throat and across her caramel-colored skin. He attempted to speak in between kisses. "I'm…sorry…I just…missed you so much…and seeing you…with that jerk—"

His mouth reached her collar bone, and he realized how close he was to the top of her dress and the tie that was holding in her breasts. Continuing his descent down her chest, he slowly began to untie the top of her dress while Maddie moaned, knotting her fists in his hair.

She struggled to talk. "We need to debrief." She cuts herself off with a moan as he freed her chest from the confines of the sundress. Palming her right breast, he took the left one in his mouth, teasing her with his tongue. "Jack." she panted, yanking on his hair hard.

He lifted his head and Maddie's mouth crashed down onto his. She splayed her palms across his chest and pushed him back, walking with him until his calves hit the toilet. Practically falling onto the seat, Maddie straddled him, cradling his face in her hands. It reminded him of the first time she visited him in his office and came on his couch.

Breaking the kiss, he kneaded her breasts again as she closed her eyes and let her head roll back. He was so hard it was almost painful, and he knew she could feel it. His bulge was right there, at the apex of her thighs and she started to move back and forth, rubbing against him. He clenched his teeth so tight he was afraid he might chip a tooth.

"Maddie if you don't stop, I might come right now."

Her eyes found his and as they focus, she smiled wickedly. Encouraged by her actions, he palmed her butt yanking her closer and stood. She wrapped her legs around his waist, and he slammed her against the wall. She gasped and her smile grew, biting her lower lip and driving him insane. He moved to unzip his pants when all of a sudden the handle on the bathroom door jiggled.

They both froze and locked eyes. Both mirroring each other, wide and surprised. The jiggling continues and Jack finally found his voice to yell, "Occupied." Slowly he caught his breath and loosened his hold on Maddie who untangled her legs from his waist, painfully sliding down his body, gently laughing.

"We got a bit carried away, didn't we?"

"That seems to happen when I'm around you." He stared as she readjusted and tied her dress, smoothing out her hair and going back to looking perfect in a matter of seconds.

He grabbed her hand bringing it to his lips. "Come over to my place? We need to go over everything that's happened."

She nodded in agreement, still not saying anything.

It took a minute for Jack to sort himself out and walk normally but when he did, they held hands and left the bar, not caring that they almost had sex in a bathroom, not caring about much because right now he had his girl back.

****

Matt had just stepped back into the shadow of the alley that was across the street from the bar when he spied Maddie leaving. Hand in hand with lover boy.

He knew it. He knew that this was too good to be true. A smile began as a plan took hold.

Chapter Twenty

Grinning like an idiot, Jack walked hand in hand with Maddie back to his apartment. It took longer than usual to get back, mostly because he kept stopping to kiss her until they remembered they stood in the middle of a busy neighborhood.

Once they were finally in the safety of his apartment, he began to pull her toward the bedroom when she planted her feet. "We need to talk about Matt first."

As much as he knew she was right, he still could not hide his disappointment and directed her to the couch. They both sat down but after a moment of hesitation, Maddie moved to the other couch, making Jack laugh.

Pulling out her cell phone, she pressed play on the recording, and they listened to it in its entirety. His blood boiled every time Matt spoke to her in a condescending way and how he'd grabbed her hand and kissed her cheek. He listened to the whole thing with eyes closed, in order to better concentrate. When the recording ended, they both sat in silence.

Jack was the first to break the silence, speaking with head still in hands. "He never actually states anything incriminating, but he does answer a few key questions. He says he 'placed the bracelet there' but it could be argued that he was speaking about another time and place." He looked up to see Maddie's crestfallen expression.

"So, you're saying that none of this is helpful?"

He quickly shook his head. "No, not at all. I am saying this will be a bit trickier than I originally thought."

He stood and began pacing the small space between the TV and coffee table. "What we need to do is transcribe this and send it and the recording to Ben. I'll do that as your attorney. I'll set up a meeting with him and try to get more information. We've both told him our suspicions about Matt so he's already on his radar..." He trailed off, looking at Maddie, who was now slumped back into the couch. Pivoting toward her, he held out his arms. "Do you need a hug?"

That earned him a laugh out of her, and she silently stood making her way into his embrace. Her arms came around his waist and he breathed in deeply, vanilla and lavender filling his senses, and squeezing tighter. "It'll be okay. I'll fix it." As she began to pull away, he knew she was about to get defensive. Tightening his hold, he added, "Not that you can't but I've got connections. You are very capable."

She looked up at him with a wicked smile. "Wanna go into your room? I could use a distraction."

Jack immediately pivoted them and steered her toward his bedroom as her phone began to vibrate. Stopping once again, he waited as she pulled her cell out of her purse and furrowed her brow. "I—its Matt."

Leaning over, Jack asked, "What did he say?" She angled the screen so they both could see. The first was a photo of Maddie's roommate Sarah and her boyfriend walking hand in hand down the steps of their apartment. As they looked, another photo appeared in the message box, this one of Steph and her boyfriend getting into a car. Finally, a text came through.

—*Looks like the roommates are gone for the night*—

Maddie pulled her eyes from the screen and looked up at Jack. "Wha-what does this mean?" Before he could theorize with her, the alert for a new message sounded out again, causing them both to look down.

—*I saw you leaving the bar with someone. Maybe I'll stay here until you get back. Wouldn't want anything bad to happen to you...or Jack*—

"He saw us," she whispered. Her hand started to tremble. "He knows I'm with you."

Jack wound his arms around her, pulling her head onto his chest. "It's okay. I'm not going to let something happen to you or your friends." He stroked her back in a soothing manner until her body stopped shaking.

She gazed up at him. "I don't know where I feel safe staying tonight." He looked down at her, studying her until an idea popped into his head.

"Want to go meet my family?"

****

While Maddie freshened up, Jack made a series of texts and phone calls. First to his abuela to tell her he was coming and bringing someone special. The squeal of excitement followed by the chiding of not giving her enough time to prepare made him smile and roll his eyes. He knew she always had a freezer of back up food at the ready and kept her place impeccable.

Next, Jack texted the guys for an impromptu hangout on the shared patio of his abuela's apartment, with a resounding yes from them all and promises of bringing beers and liquors.

Finally, he called Ben and gave him the update. Citing a "tip" Ben said he would post a black and white to drive by Maddie's neighborhood and that he would see them later.

Jack then sat on the couch and waited for Maddie. He was taking her home, to the place where he grew up. When the thought first came to mind, he felt excited. He would finally get to introduce his girl to the guys and to the most important woman in his life but now he was starting to have second thoughts. Maybe this wasn't a good environment for Maddie and Abuela Tina to meet for the first time. Maybe this time, his grandmother was being serious and didn't have the place ready for guests. Maybe—

A warm body sank into the couch next to him and cuddled into his side. He was enveloped by her vanilla scent, and he closed his eyes, letting her presence fill him with warmth.

"You sure your grandma is okay with us spending the night there? I can always find a hotel or something or sleep on the couch or I guess I can find a late train up to Michigan and stay with my parents—"

He cut her off with a kiss. "You're not leaving my sight tonight. My abuela is going to be happy to meet you and have you stay. She's going to love you."

A blush fanned across her face, making him smile.

"Come on, the car is waiting."

Chapter Twenty-One

Raucous laughter surrounds me as I bring the bottle of beer to my lips, trying—and failing—to hide my smile. Jack's grandma, or abuela as she yelled at me to call her, has been telling stories to the group sitting outside on the patio about Jack as a child, each one more embarrassing than the next.

His friends have added details here and there, much to his chagrin, but his smile has never once wavered— nor has his hand moved from my body all night. He has either held my hand, palmed my knee or draped an arm across the back of my chair. It's done nothing to subdue the butterflies in my stomach.

When we first pulled up to the apartment building up in Rogers Park, the shocked state I was previously in had subsided and all that was left was the anxiety of meeting Jack's grandmother for the first time. I've had to deal with parents of every variety at my school and could easily get a read on someone, but it had been a long while since I met someone important to the person I was dating for the first time. All the nerves melted away as soon as his abuela opened the door and threw her arms around the pair of us.

She was about my height, with thick salt and pepper hair pulled back into a ponytail. She wore a vibrant blue and green wrap dress with pink flip flops and delicate gold rings and necklaces, not at all what I expected her to look like even having seen the photo of her in his bedroom. Jack had laughed at my surprised expression as she ushered me into the living room. She lived in a cozy two-bedroom apartment with photos of various family members adorning the walls. Her arm was still wrapped around me as she yelled at Jack over her shoulder to put the bags in his old bedroom. I looked at Jack, silently wondering what we could tell her about why we were staying the night, but he took care of that. "I told you, this was last minute. We don't have any bags."

She looked offended as she shook my hand. "So, you just sprung this meeting on this poor girl? *Ay dios…*"

I placed my hand on her arm. "It's all right, really. I was down for a last-minute visit. I've been wanting to meet the woman who raised him. He has nothing but good things to say about you."

She looked at me and smiled. "I don't believe any of that, but you get points for trying to make him look good." She laughed giving me a one-armed hug. "Are you hungry? I've got some arepas and tamales…"

She continued on as she pulled me into the kitchen where the delicious smell of home cooking invaded my senses. I looked over my shoulder at Jack who followed behind, smiling and giving me a look that was making me blush.

Soon after we arrived, Jack's friends showed up and we moved our group out onto the stone patio in the back of the building. Beyond the patio was a wall of large boulders which bordered on a thin strip of sand that led out onto Lake Michigan. The farther north you went in Chicago, the more apartment buildings like this is what you would find. Homes that have been lived in by the same family for years that have managed to stay alive while high-rises were built right next store

After a few hours, his abuela decided to go in to clean and wind down for the evening, leaving us to sit and enjoy the patio and tell Jack's friends the whole story of what was going on. It was then that Ben arrived, and I immediately tensed.

Jack gave my leg a squeeze before standing and accepting a handshake from Ben as he made his way around the circle of friends. Ben got to me and stopped in his tracks, looking a bit sheepish and awkward. I nodded and he visibly relaxed before finding a seat on the other side of the circle.

"Girl, I still don't know what you see in our boy here," Marcus said, leaning back in his lawn chair. "I can assure you he's ten times better than this douchebag, Matt."

Mike laughed, adding, "Yeah, I mean, you are *way* out of his league. It must be that old school, gentlemen charm that I had to teach him. Trust me, if you had met me first—"

He is cut off by a growl coming from Jack who is giving him a hard look. "Stop ogling my girl."

Mike sits back, waving his hands in surrender. "No harm, that was a test to see how you really felt about her. I'm just trying to help her out."

That earns him a laugh from everyone, especially after I say, "Don't worry, he's been vetted by my roommates, and he passed their test. He's even managed to get himself out of hot water already."

A round of "oohhs" emits from the circle and my eyes land Ben as he looks down at his beer bottle. I hate to say that I feel a bit satisfied with his reaction toward me, now if he would just man up and apologize to my face, I think we would all be able to move on.

I glance at Jack who looks back at me with sincerity in his eyes. "Trust me, I plan on making that up to you as soon as I can." The longer we stare at each other, the more the heat builds until we are knocked from the spell by a fake retching noise.

Stevie is doubled over in his chair, pretending to vomit. "I think that should be our cue to get out of here, boys."

As all the men leave, they each give me a hug, whispering to me how good of a guy Jack is. For all the ribbing they do, they make up for in having each other's backs which I find too cute. Marcus pulls me aside when it's his turn to say goodbye. "I know Jack screwed up but he's not a bad guy. He's serious about you. I don't remember the last time he wanted us to meet someone he was seeing."

I was taken aback at that but recovered fast. "Thank you for saying that Marcus. Don't tell him but I'm pretty serious about him, too."

He grinned as he turned to leave. "Your secret is safe with me"

My matching grin was suddenly wiped from my face when Ben stopped in front of me. I looked past him at Jack who was saying goodbye to Stevie but keeping a not-so-subtle eye on the two of us.

My focus turned back to Ben who stood before me with his hands shoved in his pockets, looking me directly in the eye. "I just wanted to say I'm sorry for the texts. It was unnecessary. I'm not sorry for doing my job and protecting my friend but I am sorry for how I went about handling the situation."

I crossed my arms and blew out a breath. "I understand your reasoning and even though you deserve to be berated more, I accept your apology."

Nodding his head and offering me a slight smile, Ben turns and silently walks away.

Abuela turned Jack's old bedroom into a guestroom after he moved out. Thankfully she had the foresight to buy a full bed rather than stick with the twin that he said used to be in this small room.

I hear the door to the room click shut behind me and I am suddenly whirled around, hoisted up into the air and pressed against the wall. "I like them," I say as Jack runs his nose down the line of my neck.

"That makes me happy. They all liked you, too."

My brain is beginning to shut down as his hands, which are cupped around my bottom begin to squeeze but I am still aware his grandmother is just down the hall. "Even Ben?"

His lips now trailed down my nape, his tongue darting out and skimming my skin causing me to clench my thighs around his waist. "Mmhmm even him but can we not talk about other men while I'm trying to finish what we started earlier today?"

I struggle to breathe as I'm lifted higher, and he nips at the swell of my breast. Swallowing, I manage to find my voice, but it comes out as a quivering mess. "Jack, your abuela is in the next room." His head lifts and his hazel eyes sparkle. "Then I guess you're going to have to be quiet."

I'm suddenly dropped to my feet and spun around to face the wall as the skirt of my dress gets pushed up from behind. "Ever since you walked into that bar, I've been wanting to do this." His hand slips between my legs, fingers pushing aside my already soaked underwear and work their way into me. My eyes roll back and a loud moan begins to work its way past my lips when his other hand clamps over my mouth.

"Didn't I just tell you to be quiet? You don't want to be interrupted by someone walking in, would you?"

I pant and shake my head as his fingers move against the bundle of nerves inside me, working me into a frenzy. Jack pushes the length of his body against mine, pinning me in place against the wall and I can honestly say I've never been more aroused.

Suddenly the warmth of his fingers is gone, and I make a noise of protest before I recognize the sound of a zipper. The next moment, I feel him probe my entrance as his hot breath tickles the shell of my ear. "I haven't stopped thinking about you since I had you."

He thrusts into me and my fingers scratch at the wall, desperate for something to hold onto as I whimper in pleasure. I push back into him as he continues his relentless claiming of my body. His voice murmurs in my ear, "I have been miserable without you. I've missed you so much, needed you." His hand moves from mouth to my neck, pinning me harder as I begin to arch my back. "I'm never letting you go again." I feel the scruff of his cheek against my temple and my hand flies back, tangling in his hair as I turn my face toward his.

"Good."

His pupils dilate and he somehow thrusts deeper into me as his lips cover mine, tongue plunging into my mouth. I bite his lip hard as the hand that's not pinning me, slides around and plays with my clit, sending me into ecstasy with him following right after.

He slumps into me, and I welcome the weight of him

against me while simultaneously pinning me against the wall, holding me up as my legs stopped working a while ago. We attempt to abate our panting and at some point he peels himself from me, gently turns me around and scoops me into his arms.

I'm so spent that I don't even mind him carrying me the few feet to the bed. I can't look away from him as he gently places me down and lies next to me. It's such a contrast from the passion of a few moments ago that I feel overwhelmed with emotion. He scoots in so that our noses are almost touching. Looking at each other, neither of us speaks, having a silent understanding of something that I can't put into words. My eyes flutter closed and laying there in the arms of Jack with his fingers grazing my back, I manage to forget about all the problems that await us and fall asleep.

****

I woke with a delicious ache below my waist and a smile on my face. I could feel the steady rise and fall of Jack's chest behind me and have a momentary flashback of the last time I woke up with him. I expect to feel panic, some sort of PTSD but none of that comes my way. I look over my shoulder to find Jack's intense hazel eyes staring at me. "You know some would call this creepy."

My voice is raspy from sleep, but I can't hide the amusement in my words. "Well, are any of those people here right now?"

"Nope."

He flashes his pearly whites at me, and I feel my insides melt. He leans in and brushes his lips against mine, cupping my face in his large palm. "I like waking up with you."

I giggle. "Me, too. Now get up and make me

breakfast."

He snorts and tilts my head up. "If you don't think my abuela has been up for half an hour already, banging around in the kitchen, you are seriously mistaken." He presses another quick kiss to my lips before rolling over and off the bed.

The rest of the morning goes by fast. We enjoyed a wonderful breakfast and say an elongated goodbye as his grandma kept bribing me with more food to stay longer. Finally, Jack had to literally wave his phone in her face, proving that our car was waiting and that we had to leave. On the off chance Matt was still watching my place, we decided to head to my apartment so that I wouldn't be alone.

Ben had advised us to stay there and see if any contact was made. By six o'clock that night, nothing had happened. Jack and I lay in my bed with my feet on his lap as he gave me a foot massage.

"You keep rubbing my feet like this and I'm never letting you leave," I groan as he worked a knot out of my arch.

"You don't have to worry about that for tonight at least. I'm definitely staying over." When his phone buzzed, he paused his massage to read a text from Ben out loud. "I've officially got Matt on surveillance. It's not twenty-four-seven, but it should help."

Sighing, I accepted his words. Jack and I spent the rest of the night curled up in bed together.

Life feels like it's getting back to normal. That is, if you consider normal being the suspect in a robbery and knowing that your ex-boyfriend is behind it. That's what being back with Jack is like though, making everything else feel normal.

****

After the night in Rogers Park, he and I have either seen each other or spoken to each other every day. It's nice to be reminded of this feeling, this relationship stuff. The feeling of wanting to tell that person all the random things that happen to you throughout the day, that you want to hear their voice right before you go to bed, that you want to just be with them all the time. I've had to jolt myself back into reality a few times when I found myself daydreaming about moving in with him or meeting his family. Just because I was mentally nesting with him didn't mean he was.

Today, I am lounging on my patio with my phone pressed to my ear while Jack, who is walking home from work, tells me about his day.

"You wouldn't believe the amount of running around I did today. From now on I'm making my clients come to me but at least I got to see Ben—" He abruptly cut himself off.

His friend and the ensuing investigation were topics we've tried to avoid when we are in what we call "couple mode." I think it's mostly because he doesn't want to remind me of how mad I got at him.

"I'm glad you brought him up," I say. "Has he said anything about the recording?"

"He did but…since you were kind of agreeing with Matt, it doesn't cast you in a good light."

"Good light? I was playing along! Does he not understand the meaning of *undercover*?"

There is a rustling on the other end, and I can picture him balancing his phone while trying to unlock the door to his apartment. Once he's in, I hear him switch me to the speaker function as he moves around.

"I know but I'm just worried in the future this will be used against you. There are certain procedures Ben needs to take before he can fully move it up the chain."

"He hasn't even moved it up the chain yet or whatever that means?"

"I mean he's showed it to his boss but went no higher than that."

I sigh deeply and rub my forehead. "Jack, we can't keep putting this off. We need to do something. Especially because Matt reached out to me again and he's being a bit more insistent on talking to me." My voice is beginning to ramp higher and sound more panicked. "What if he comes over here again? Or what if he plants more evidence? Or what if—"

Jack switches me off speaker and interrupts me, his voice is soothing in my ear. "Take a deep breath. I'll call Ben immediately and then I'm coming over there. Let me change super quick and then I'll—"

He suddenly stops talking and the phone goes so silent I think the call might have dropped.

"Jack?"

His voice comes back a whisper. "I know this sounds crazy, but I think someone is picking my lock."

Cold fear washes over my body and now I'm whispering, "Hide. Get out of there. Do something but stay on the phone."

"I'm grabbing my bat."

I hear shuffling on the other end and a small "clink" as he places the phone down on what I can only assume is his dresser. My knuckles are white as I grip the edge of the lounger I'm sitting on as I strain to hear anything from the other end. The faint sound of a doorknob slowly turning and clicking lets me know that where he set his phone is right next to the bedroom door. My breathing becomes shallower as to not make any sound.

"*Hey.*"

It's farther away from the phone but I can make out Jack's voice. A crash and a grunt ring out followed by an "*Ahh.*" More crashing and thuds sound out, and my heart is practically jumping out of my chest, it's beating so fast. Suddenly an eerie silence fills the end of the line.

I'm shaking as I whisper, "Jack?"

I can make out footsteps and again say his name, this time saying it louder, but what greets me on the other end of the phone makes me sick to my stomach.

"Hello, Maddie."

It's Matt.

Chapter Twenty-Two

As my fingers lose feeling, the phone almost drops out of my hand. Tightening my grip on the cell, I run into the apartment from the patio in a panic and find Sarah and Stephanie sitting on the couch. The look on my face causes them to jump up but I wave my hand, and put my finger to my lips in warning.

Placing the phone on speaker mode, I say, "Matt, what are you doing at Jack's apartment?"

"Maddie, you know what I'm doing here and I'm going to need you to join me soon or I'm worried something might happen to your boyfriend, or is it ex still? I couldn't tell your relationship status when I saw the two of you leaving the bar the other night."

While my roommates' eyes go wild with confusion, I attempt to control my breathing. "I don't understand."

He lets out a mirthless chuckle. "We're one person short of a group, and I'll need some help, especially from someone who knows the building as well as you do. So be a good girl, hop in a cab, and come over."

"Where is Jack?"

"He's sitting right next to me, but my patience is wearing thin, Maddie. He managed to hurt two of my friends, but we got in a few hits."

My stomach churns at the thought of loser Matt and his friends laying their hands on Jack. I look up from the phone at my roommates and they're both shaking their heads no. "Put him on the phone first. I want to make sure he's okay"

Grunts echo through the speaker before I hear an angry but weakened voice say, "I'm all right."

Just hearing those two words bring tears to my eyes. "Jack, I'm so sorry"

"Maddie don't come—"

Jack is cut off abruptly as Matt comes back on the line. "I'll see you here soon." The phone disconnects and my breath catches in my throat.

I look up. We all stay silent for a moment before all hell breaks loose. I turn and run to my room to grab my purse, Stephanie starts yelling at me to call the police and Sarah is ripping cushions off the couch in an attempt to find her phone.

As I shove random things into my bag, Stephanie's hand shoots out and grips my wrist. "You're not seriously thinking of going there, are you?"

Wrenching my arm away, I say, "Of course I am but I'm not going alone." I'm able to stop shaking long enough pick up my cell to order a carshare ride to Jack's building.

I look up in time to see Sarah has found her phone and she's yelling, "I'm calling 9-1-1 now."

Moving faster than I have in a long time, I jump and slap her phone from her hand, sending it to the carpet. "No, I have a plan. I'll call Ben on the way there."

I rush to the door; both of them run up behind me and Stephanie continues to shout, "Are you crazy? Don't you want to wait and see what the professionals say before you rush into a place where your crazy ex-boyfriend is holding your current boyfriend hostage with probably a weapon?"

"I'm going. It's happening. I'll be fine." Twisting to run down the stairs, I pause and turn back around. "Both of you should stay with your boyfriends tonight. I don't want either of you here alone."

Without another word and giving them a chance to stop me, I run out the door and down the stairs, away from their cries of objection. Quickly getting into the awaiting car, I begin to dial Ben's number but then stop.

I need to clear my head and go over everything first.

Okay, my suspicions were correct, and Matt and his gang of dummies are robbing upscale apartment buildings on the Gold Coast. They get someone on the inside to learn about the building and its layout and routines, then strike. They've hit two apartments in Jack's building already but I don't think they've ever done it there before. From what I've read, they hit one apartment in a building and move on.

That tells me they clearly want something else here. The latest break-in looked more violent, angry, they're escalating—but I'm not sure why.

I look down and see I've accidentally opened my web app, the *MFyT* page open. I automatically start scrolling through and my eyes land on the newest post.

History of Bugging

No, not insects but listening devices! Murder Heads, we've all seen that one scene in every cop show or movie where they tape the wire to the guy's chest and they go over the rules and safe words and such but how the heck did that even start?

Back in 1906...

I stop reading and immediately call Ben.

"Hello?"

"Jack is in trouble. Matt is there at his place. I'm

going over there now."

"Whoa, wait what? Start from the beginning."

"It was Matt all along. I was right. I'm pretty sure he hurt Dan from the front desk and he's in Jack's apartment now and he's going to hurt him unless I go over there so…" I lose steam in the middle of my sentence as the adrenaline begins to wear off. "Oh my God, what am I doing?"

Ben's voice is hard and fast over the phone. "Okay, I need you to breathe and tell me everything now."

Taking a deep breath, I quickly go over everything I know, when I get to the end I say, "I'm going, and you can't stop me."

"Maddie, you don't know what you're doing. Let the police handle this."

"If he hurt an innocent man like Dan, what do you think he'll do to Jack? I'm going."

"I'm mobilizing police now and we'll be at the building soon.

"No," I yell into the phone with such force, the driver of my car swerves. Shooting him an apologetic look I continue. "I can't let them know I called you. Can you be more…I don't know, covert maybe?"

"Maddie," he says, "that's not—"

I have an idea. "Ben, come to the building, I'll leave the cell's speaker on. You'll be able to hear or record everything that happens. As soon as I get him to…I don't know, verbally admit it, you come in and save the day."

As my car pulls up to Jack's building, Ben says, "Maddie that's not how this works."

"Well, it's going to have to be because I'm here. I hope you stay on the line because I'm going in."

I turn down the volume so I can't hear Ben's voice

anymore and lock my phone screen. I begin to slip the device into my pocket but stop and slip it into my bra. This way the speaker is closer to our mouths and the sound will hopefully be less muffled. Hopping out of the car, I walk on shaky legs through the front doors of the building. The golden lobby is not busy. There is one man sitting behind the desk who barely looks up as I pass by. I don't really want to talk to anyone; I'm a bundle of nerves as I walk onto the elevator.

I don't really know what to expect when I get up there and I repeat my half-baked plan to myself as the elevator propels me up. I'm going to go to Jack's apartment. I'm going to make sure he's okay. I'm going to talk to Matt and hopefully get him to talk to me… what if he wants me to get rid of my phone? I quickly check the phone isn't poking out from the vee neckline of my shirt and whisper, "I hope someone can hear me but I'm about to enter the apartment."

The elevator doors slide open and I see the hallway is empty. I slowly make my way to Jack's door and softly knock. There is shuffling on the other side before it swings opens and I'm greeted by a smirking Matt.

"Glad you could come by." His hand wraps around my arm and pulls me quickly inside. Behind me, the click of the door locking is as loud as a slam.

I don't recognize three of the men who are standing inside Jack's apartment. Two have bruises blooming on their faces; the other is massaging and rotating his arm. I inwardly rejoice that Jack put up a fight and got some hits in. My eyes scan the room, but I don't see the man I'm most worried about.

"Where is he?"

"Don't you want to hear what we need you to do?"

I stay stony-faced and hope my voice doesn't quiver. "No. Where is he, Matt?"

He strolls over to Jack's bedroom door and opens it to show me a figure bound and gagged. As I step closer, the light from the hallway helps me to make out what exactly is in the darkened room. Jack's wrists are tied together in front of him with some rope and his mouth is gagged with a necktie. His eyes go wide, he makes some muffled sounds and starts to get up. Matt's hand begins to move to my arm again but before he gets a grip I'm running into the room.

My hands tear at the knot holding the tie in place as I try to hold back tears. "Are you hurt?" My voice comes out as a shaky whisper as I finally get the gag down and out of his mouth.

His eyes are wide and keep shifting from my face to just over my shoulder. "You should not be here, are you crazy? Run. Now."

I can't help but let out a relived chuckle and small smile as I hold his head in my hands. "You're the crazy one if you thought I wasn't going to come for you." I hug him, positioning my mouth next to his ear. "I'm recording this. I've got a plan."

He looks concerned but I turn around to Matt before he gets a chance to say anything more. "Okay, I'm here. What do you want me to do?"

"First things first. Give me your phone."

Dread fills the pit of my stomach, but I keep my face as neutral as possible. "I didn't bring it."

Matt smirks and moves toward me quickly, shoving his hands in my pockets. I try to slap them away, but he uses his body to push me against the wall, pinning me in place. Jack stands, attempting to rush forward but his hands are still bound. One of Matt's goons pops out of nowhere and holds him back.

"Get your hands off her."

I inwardly smirk as a scowl covers Matt's face after he comes up empty. The inward celebration is short lived, however, when his eyes drift down and a grin appears.

"Aw, it's like you wanted me to find it."

Faster than I thought it possible for him to move, his hand dives down the collar of my shirt causing me to yelp and Jack to thrash against his captors' hands, his face turning red.

I attempt to push him away as I feel the back of his hand against my chest but the damage is done. He grabs the phone from inside my bra. Luckily, he doesn't look at the screen before he turns and chucks it against the wall, shattering it.

"You're lucky I paid for insurance on that thing." He spins so fast that I flinch; my back hits the wall again.

"After we're done Maddie, you can get as many phones as you want." He brings his hand up to my face and lightly strokes my cheek. "Let's go sit down."

I don't bother to hide my revulsion. "I'm not going anywhere without Jack."

Matt raises one eyebrow, then turns and grabs Jack by the back of the shirt and gives him a hard shove through the door. Jack stumbles into the back of the couch, almost losing his balance. I rush forward to steady him and help him around the furniture to sit down.

"I'm okay," he says, in a voice so quiet I can barely hear him.

I brush the hair out of his eyes and run my hand gently over his head, feeling the large lump, most likely attributed to one of the goons standing before me. In the light of the room, I can see a bruise forming over his right eye and a small cut around his temple. "You *are* hurt. I'm so sorry."

"Do you know who lives on the top floor of this building?"

Our attention is pulled back to Matt, who comes over to sit on the coffee table directly in front of the couch. "It's a company-leased apartment for a big law firm. They keep it for visiting clients or for when the partners want to be alone with a special someone. Because important people stay there, they keep it looking pretty snazzy, real art, expensive baubles, the works."

"How do you know this?"

"Because we've had this gig going for a while now. When you get someone on your team to be the inside man, you learn a lot—like who lives where, who has keys to what…" He trails off and gives me a knowing look.

I swallow hard. Jack turns to me, confused. "What does that have to do with you?"

"Wait," I say. "What does that have to do with me, Matt? If you have a guy who works at this building, that means you have keys. Why would you need mine?"

Jack, still looking at me whispers incredulously, "Why do you have a key?"

"I get one every summer since Dan and I go way back. It's just easier this way for me when I come here to walk my dogs. And now is not really the time to be explaining this," I say hurriedly.

He looks exasperated and stage whispers, "This certainly doesn't help the legal case, Maddie."

"Enough." Our heads snap back to Matt who now

looks annoyed. "Watching the two of you is exhausting. And to answer your previous question, it turns out that Kent wasn't able to get the other skeleton key. That old man really took his job too seriously…"

Anger flashes in my eyes at the mention of Dan. "After you failed to intimidate some old man and messed up your plans, you idiots thought I would help you out?"

He chuckles, giving me a sly smile that makes my skin crawl. "It's why I grabbed one of your bracelets and put it in the apartment next door. The police now think you're in on this. I tried to reason with you, knowing you and I would be a good partnership. When that didn't seem to convince you, I enlisted the help of your friend Jack here. So, you would be more willing to help us."

I throw out my hand pointing a finger at him. "I knew you framed me. You're not that sneaky."

Jack puts his bound hands on my thigh in a comforting gesture but keeps his eyes trained on Matt. "I'll come with you, just let her go."

Matt preens like a kid who just won the grand prize and the fair. "We have someone watching the security cameras. And, we have experience being in and out within minutes. Plus, we have a hostage, and we have a way out thanks to some back stair surveillance and the strategically placed garage of this building. I've gone over this plan one hundred times. We'll be in and out. Jack will stay here while Maddie escorts us upstairs."

I straighten at the mention of my name, Jack's hands squeeze my thigh. "No, she will not."

I place my hand over his and say, "Why don't I just give you the key and you can leave both of us here? I'll slow you down anyways."

Matt just continues grinning and shaking his head

but then one of his goons speaks up behind him. "Dude, let's just pick her up on the way back. We'll be faster without them."

"Pick me up?" I ask incredulously. "I'll go upstairs with you but I'm not like, leaving here. I'd rather walk across broken glass then go anywhere with you idiots."

Matt leans forward and places his hand on my knee. When I try to shake it off, he grips harder. "People like him—" He nods toward Jack "—people who live in buildings like this, it's not who you belong with. He doesn't know you, doesn't understand you, what you've been through. He's had it easy, we haven't. For God's sakes we walk dogs just to get by. If you think you're ever going to be happy with a guy like that, you're mistaken. We were together for a while, and I didn't know what I had until it was gone but you and me? We're good together and now we can live a much more comfortable life with each other. We can stop working so hard and coming up empty and just go travel and live. I couldn't provide for you before but now I can, now I can treat you right."

"You're joking, right? You think that's why we weren't happy before? You're blaming you being a terrible partner on the fact that you didn't have enough money to *provide* for me?"

I don't even realize that I'm standing now and looming over Matt's still sitting form. "You are delusional if you think I want to get back together with you for any reason because, news flash, Matt, no amount of money will ever make you less shitty. You're a bad person and Jack Delgado is better than you in every single way. Hell, it's only been a few weeks but I'm more certain that I love him now than I was with you after a year!"

I'm breathing hard and glaring at him when I realize what I just said. Before I can turn though, I see the fire in Matt's eyes as he stands and makes a move to grab me but before he can, Jack jumps up.

"Enough." He slams his fists into Matt's jaw, who goes falling to the side. The three men, who were just standing across the room, run and pull Jack back. The one I recognize, Kent, holds him while another punches him in the face.

"Stop." I leap up and grab the man's fist, cocked back to hit again. He tries to shake me off, but I hold his arm with all my strength. Then I remember there is a third crony.

His hands wind around my waist and yank me off my feet, dragging me away. Matt is back on his feet, casually wiping the blood away from his lip. "That wasn't very nice." He walks over and yanks up the gag back into Jack's mouth, then proceeds to hit him in the stomach.

I scream but Crony Number Three's hand covers my mouth, muffling the sound. The guys let go of Jack and he doubles over in pain, trying to catch his breath. The room falls silent with the exception of Jack coughing and wheezing and I faintly hear it, the sound of a dog in the distance yapping due to the noise we've made. Are Mrs. Marlow and Charlie back in their apartment? Hope swells inside my chest.

I bite at the hand clamped over my mouth. He lets go with a yelp but keeps one arm around my waist. Wiping my mouth, I say, "Please Matt, stop. Look I'll leave willingly with you guys, just stop hurting him, please. Let me say goodbye.

Everyone in the room looks at me, including Jack, his watered eyes wide and pleading.

Matt rubs his knuckles and smirks. "I knew you'd see reason. We'll leave in a few minutes."

Chapter Twenty-Three

I help Jack back to the bedroom and shut the door before one of those goons follows us inside. "I'll be out in a moment. Just give us some privacy," I yell through the door while maneuvering Jack onto the bed. I gently remove the gag and cup his face in my hands, trying to remain calm and clear-headed.

"Are you okay?"

"Do not go with them."

I drop my hands and begin to untie them. He says, "Don't bother, they'll just retie them when you leave."

"Do you have anything small and sharp? We'll put it in your pocket and when they leave you alone you can start to work yourself free."

Standing, I start hurriedly going through drawers and shelves in his room, as I lower my voice. "Ben knows what's going on, they should be here soon, he heard everything until the phone broke. You're going to be okay. I'm going to be fine. I'll stall them, make noise so people hear, do whatever I can..."

I'm rambling as I continue to search for anything that will help. I feel my panic begin to well up in my chest again.

"Maddie."

He says my name so calmly that I stop and turn around. He's standing at the foot of the bed, looking at me with sad eyes. He walks over to me, puts his hands under my chin and leans in, planting a kiss on my lips.

His lips touch mine and just for a moment, everything feels okay. We are just a guy and a girl, making up after a fight, kissing in his bedroom. He pulls back and I feel overwhelmed, tears spring to my eyes as my hands come up to cup his face.

"What they said out there isn't true. I know you and I understand you and while I don't want you to go, I know you're going to anyway." His voice is soft and steady and is the only thing keeping me from having a meltdown at this moment. "It also seems like Matt still has feelings for you which leads me to believe he won't hurt you. I think you just try and stall them long enough for Ben to get here."

I try to steady my breathing as I feel a tear escape down my cheek. He brushes it away, then strokes my hair. "You'll be okay. I'll make sure of it. If anyone touches you, I swear I'll—"

I lean in and cut him off with a kiss. He winces because I've kissed him too hard and I start to pull back when he grips my chin, not letting me. He kisses me back with such ferocity that my toes curl, but it's quickly cut short when a pounding on the door ends the moment.

"We're leaving now."

I push him to the side and quickly go into his bathroom. It takes me a moment to find a pair of nail clippers which I grab and walk back, placing it in his palm.

"I meant what I said out there…about my feelings." I take a deep breath. "Don't say anything now. Just…I don't care what he thinks, you and I will be very happy together."

Taking one last look into those hypnotic hazel eyes,

I turn and open the door to leave the bedroom.

****

Jack watched as Maddie left the room, the door closing behind her. Standing up from the bed and wincing at the soreness in his abs from the hits he took, he pressed his ear to the door to make out the male voices.

"...fifteen minutes...clean up."

The nail clippers were still warm in his palm, but he tossed them onto the bed and rushed to his closet. He kept a Swiss army knife in a small box. Grabbing it, he began cutting the ties around his wrists. It seemed to take forever but he steadily continued until he managed to get his hands free.

He had only used up a few minutes, he estimated that he had ten more left before Kent needed to "clean up" so he needed to be quick. The tablet in his nightstand was thankfully charged and Jack messaged Ben on it, typing as fast and clear as possible, telling him who was here, and that Maddie was with the other.

He got a response immediately.

—We've got people outside surrounding the building, trying not to tip them off. Get to a safe space and barricade yourself in—

Frustration swelled. He couldn't just stay there; he had to go get Maddie. When she professed her love for him to Matt, he hadn't allowed himself to think about it, choosing to instead focus on keeping her safe but now...

It's only been a short time, but he was crazy in love with Maddie...The tablet buzzed, snapping him out of his reverie.

—Don't do what you're thinking. Let us handle it—

Wow, Ben really knew him well. Jack did not

hesitate to respond.

—Sorry, brother—

When he heard the group breaking into his apartment the first time, he used his baseball bat as protection. Now the only object at his disposal was a souvenir Cubs bat he got when he was twelve. Gripping it tight, he took a deep breath and slowly opened the door of his bedroom just enough to see out.

Kent was standing at the window and luckily his back was to him. Opening the door farther, Jack made his way out into the living room as quietly as possible. Inching closer to Kent, he raised the small bat in hand, then hesitated. What if he hit him too hard? What if he did more harm than just knock him out? What would the legal implications of this—

He realized his mistake in hesitating and not turning off his lawyer-trained brain as Kent turned around, his eyes growing wide in surprise. Jack swung the bat, smacking him with it on the left side of his face. Kent's eyes rolled back in his head. His body fell against the window then slid to the floor.

A moment of panic set in as Jack checked for a pulse. Feeling relief that he didn't kill the bastard, he rushed into his room to grab a necktie to bind his hands. The first part of the plan was done and now he just had to figure out how to get to the penthouse.

Chapter Twenty-Four

As the elevator rises to the top floor, I produce the key that will give us access to the penthouse. I stand in the back and size up the men in front of me as we all wait in silence. They're all of a similar build to Matt, tall and muscular.

"So, where did you guys all meet?"

I'm met with glares from all three.

"Can't be dog walkers, I haven't seen you guys before. Must be losers who hang out at bars and have no jobs because why else would you rob innocent people?"

Big goon on the left turns toward me but Matt throws out a hand, stopping him from doing anything further. I smirk and say in the most condescending voice I can muster, "Oh, that must've hit a nerve."

"Maddie, stop being difficult." Matt barks, still facing forward. I'm about to say something snarky in return but just then the elevator doors open.

I've never been up here before and am taken aback to see not a hallway but the actual condo. White marble tiles on the floor blend into pristine white walls and a small chandelier hangs above. The atrium opens up a few feet away, giving ways to a large sitting room complete with three couches and a grand piano. This is the type of place you see in a show where a swanky cocktail party would take place...or where a corrupt boss brings his mistress on a lunch break. I remind myself that when this is done, I need to consume more comedies and Chic-Lit books and take a break from crime novels and mafia romances.

We all walk out slowly, taking in our surroundings until Matt, ever the leader, snaps us back to attention. "Okay, five minutes. Joe, you take the bedrooms. Kyle, you take any offices. Maddie and I'll do the big areas."

The goons produce tiny bundles of fabric from their jacket pockets, and I realize they're thin duffle bags. They run off but I stand there and cross my arms. "*We* are not doing anything. I don't want to rob people; I want to leave and help the police catch you."

His large hand wraps around my bicep and yanks hard, causing me to stumble after him into the large living room.

"You will do what I tell you or Kent might rid the world of one more lawyer."

"Screw you."

Matt pulls on my arm, bringing my body uncomfortably close to his. "You already did, remember?" He grins.

I remember when I used to find that humor and grin charming, now all I want to do is slap it off his face. "You're right, I did. Thank God I don't have to do it anymore. I was getting tired of faking it."

His other hand grabs the back of my head and forces it toward him. "Maybe I should remind you."

Until this moment, I haven't actually been scared. Maybe anxious, nervous, angry but now I'm afraid of what he could try and do to me.

His lips come crashing down on me and I begin clawing and hitting him, attempting to extricate myself but he holds me hard. I attempt to knee him but we're so close together that I only get as far as his thigh. Luckily, I put enough force to it to surprise him which is all I need to manage to get away from him.

I push him and back away, looking for anything to use as a weapon and my hands somehow land on a large, crystal elephant figure. I grasp it tight and hold it in front of me, trying to get something in between us. He lets out a sinister laugh and moves toward me.

I wait until he gets close enough and then I strike, sending the figurine in the area of his head. He dodges but not fast enough and I clip his shoulder, hard. He stumbles, his hand going to his shoulder.

Goon Number Two, Joe I think, comes running back into the room, his duffle bag practically busting at the seams with stolen items. "Matt, what are you doing? Leave her alone and hurry up."

Something akin to a growl escapes Matt's lips as he glares at his friend and then spins around, rifling through the knick-knacks around the room. Number Two drops his bag by the elevator and speeds into the kitchen area. No one is looking at me. Can I make it to the elevator?

I begin to inch toward the direction of the hallway when Matt says, "Don't even think about it." He didn't even turn around.

Still gripping my elephant, I turn, ignoring him and hurry down the hallway not toward the elevator but the rooms. All the doors are open and I glance in as I pass them. There are multiple bedrooms, now trashed, with dresser drawers pulled out. A bathroom, which of course has a smashed mirror. Mental note to ask them about that later. An entertainment room of sorts, again with smashed screens and upended furniture. At the very end of the hall is an office.

I look over my shoulder and see the men still running around so I take the opportunity to slip quietly into the room. I close and lock the door, thinking I can barricade myself in or at least slow them down. I turn around to take stock of my surroundings. Everything is scattered, with most of the mess on top of a large mahogany desk. Papers, books, folders, I attempt to sift through everything to find a landline I can use. I spot the black plastic handle and am dismayed to see the cord has been cut.

Suddenly a low male voice calls out, "It's time."

I hear shuffling and then the doorknob is rattling. I dive under the desk to hide as I hear a body slam against the door and the wooden frame cracking. Loud, angry footsteps come close and soon a hand shoots under the desk where I hide, pulling me out and up onto my feet. Goon Number One appears and looks at me expectantly.

I back up to the window. Looking down on the street, I don't see any flashing lights or cop cars. Is this good or bad? Ben wouldn't have ignored the call so they're either not here yet or they're not showing themselves. I'm hoping it's the second one and that they'll pop out or something when we get down to the street.

Goon Number One is walking toward me. "Let's. Go. Now."

Panic sets in, what can I do to either delay or stop them from getting away?

A glass bowl is sitting on the windowsill next to me, filled with potpourri. Without thinking I turn my back to him and quickly shove my hand in it and stuff my pockets with the dried leaves. Maybe I can leave a trail, and someone will find us once we're downstairs. His hand wraps around my bicep and I am physically removed from the room.

****

On the phone with Ben, Jack paced the length of his living room, being careful not to trip over the still unconscious Kent. "No one has come in or out yet. I'm telling you, they're still in there."

Ben's voice was calm yet stern. He was good in a crisis, which is probably why he's such a good cop, despite his height and good-natured face, he has always been able to command any situation and keep things on track. Jack could tell he was on his last nerve with him however, as he kept asking the same things over and over again.

"Well then, let me just come out there so I can be there when Maddie gets out—"

"No, we've been over this. I don't want you to have a run in with them by chance on their way out and mess up the plans. Stay put."

"I am going out of my mind here. If I had a way to access that penthouse, I'd be up there now, no matter what you say."

"I know man. I know."

There was a pause before Ben spoke again. "I will contact you the second I see her."

Jack mumbled a thanks and hung up. He looked down at the man propped against the wall, he was going to have one hell of a headache when he woke up. The lump was already forming on the side of his head. Jack kind of wanted to wake him up, see if he could get any information out of him. While contemplating this, standing in the middle of his apartment, he heard a faint noise come from the hallway. Was that the elevator?

Rushing to the door, he was about to open it when Ben's warning rang in his ears. If it was them and he stepped out, they might change their course of action. They might hurt Maddie. Rather than open it, he pressed his ear to the door, trying to hear what was going on in the hall.

"…Kent…here"

"He knows…problem."

Well, they already knew something was wrong if Kent was supposed to be waiting out in the hallway for them. Suddenly a higher voice speaks.

"Let me…here"

Jack could hear the doors close and silence, once again, filled the hallway. He counted to five and when he continued to hear nothing, cautiously opened the door. Throwing a glance back at the still sleeping thug, he walked into the hallway, toward the closed metal doors.

It was so small he almost missed it but in the corner, next to the door is a small flower petal. He picked it up, bringing it closer to inspect and the smell was strong. It was potpourri. He glanced around but already knew there was nothing that lived in this hallway that resembled this. So how did it get here?

Running back into the apartment, he grabbed his phone and the normal sized baseball bat that was taken from him, before closing the door and going to the stairwell.

He began the journey down the stairs, happy he only lived on the eighth floor. Ignoring the burn from the bruises on his torso, he was propelled on by adrenaline. By the time he arrived at the fifth floor, he heard the echoes of a door opening down below. Pausing in his descent, he stopped and listened to the voice that echoed up the stairwell.

"Matt, please—"

"Maddie, shut the hell up before I shut you up."

His blood boiled as he began walking again, as quietly as possible. Suddenly he heard another door open; the voices and steps were cut off.

Resuming his quick pace, he made it down to the second floor only to find a few more potpourri petals. He smiled.

It's a trail.

And Maddie was leaving him breadcrumbs.

Chapter Twenty-Five

When Kent wasn't waiting when the elevator doors opened, the smug air evaporated from the elevator.

I was surprised when the elevator stopped again, this time on the third floor, and we exited, heading for the stairwell. I was even more surprised when we exited that stairwell on the second floor and made our way to a door that said *Employees Only*.

Through that door another stairwell went down, this one more narrow and dirtier. Throughout this quick journey, I've been able to scatter a few petals here and there. At first, it was more for someone to come find me but now, going down this unfamiliar way, it's to help me get back if I get away.

When. When I get away. I remind myself.

We head down the stairway and come out into the wide, vaulted garage and I can't help but snort. "So, you're just walking out through the garage? That's your big getaway?"

"Not quite. Our way out is over here."

I stop walking, making Matt stop and turn as well. "Let's go," he says and man, he is angry.

"*Our* way? Matt when can I leave?"

"Once we're across the state line." He turns to continue walking but again, I keep my feet rooted to the spot. "You never said anything about leaving the city. Let me go now. You haven't told me your destination, so

I won't be able to tell the cops. Just knock me out or something and leave me here."

Matt's fingers tighten over my arm. "Not a chance, Mads. You're coming with me until we get free and clear of the city." He pulls hard enough to make me stumble against his chest. I need to tilt my head up to continue trying to stare him down. "Once you get away from here with me, you'll be happier. You'll love Indiana."

He clearly doesn't know me at all. I have never been a fan of Indiana.

I try to pull my arm away but he quickly let's go and bends down, wrapping an arm around my legs. He hoists me over his shoulder in a fireman's carry. Banging my fists as hard as I can on his back and screaming do me no good as he walks toward the door, his body oblivious to my abuse.

He pauses and I hear grunting from one of his friends and the sound of a heavy door scrape against the concrete floor. Trying not to panic at not being able to move, I try to unearth the last petals in my pocket and scatter them as we go through the door.

"What was that?"

The blood drains from my face as Matt puts me down. I get a head rush as I take in my surroundings. We've entered another stairwell, this one even more narrow and dark than the last.

"What did you drop?"

"Nothing, how could I when you grabbed me like a fricking ape?"

"What. Did. You. Drop?" His voice is low and eerily calm. I back up only to have the wall meet me in such a small space. He crowds me, looming over my small frame.

"Matt, let's go."

His friends are already halfway down the stairs, looking back in concern. One of them looks like he wants to intercede which makes me even more nervous.

"You trying to leave a trail of breadcrumbs Maddie?"

"Matt, back off." My command would sound better if my voice wasn't coming out shaking.

"Do you know what I told Kent to do before we left? I told him to clean up the mess we made in Jack's apartment. Told him to make sure this time it's not a coma that's the end result."

My stomach drops. I gave Jack a way to break out. He's smart and strong. He's fine. He has to be fine. He's not going to be *cleaned up* by Kent. Rage causes me to shake which Matt mistakes for fear. "You don't have anything to go back to, Maddie. You're coming with us."

"No, I'm not." Being against the wall, I don't have much room to wind my fist back so I attempt an uppercut and punch him as hard as I can in the chin. Luckily, the element of surprise is on my side.

He lets out a scream, drops his bag with a loud clang and grips his face in pain.

I stumble to the door and try to unlock it but I'm shaking so bad, my fingers can't work as quickly. His palm lands on my shoulder, spinning me around on the spot. My instincts take over as I shove him with all my might. He's taken by surprise again and is thrown off balance as he slams into the adjacent wall. I turn to try and go back through the now closed door, but his hands are around my waist pulling me away.

I swing my elbow back and it makes contact with his stomach, knocking the air out of him. Doubled over, his arms leave me, and I take the opportunity to spin around and push him again, this time there is no wall behind him, instead the narrow staircase. He flies back, landing on his friends as the three lose their balance and tumble down the stairs.

I'm momentarily frozen in place as the fear takes over. I know they're bad and they're trying to hurt me but part of me wants to check if they're okay. I've listened to enough stories to know a fall down the stairs can be deadly. After a moment I hear groaning and that's all I need to break me out of my trance and turn back to the door.

It's a heavy, metal door that, at first, does not budge. After pulling a few times, it begins to slide open. I look over my shoulder and see the outline of the three men in the dim light, untangling themselves from each other.

I place my foot on the wall next to the handle and use my whole weight to get the door open wide enough for me to fit through. I shimmy my body through the opening; one foot, head, shoulders, hips and lastly my other foot...which gets caught.

I look back and yell in surprise as I see a hand wrapped around my ankle. I give a violent kick which results in smacking my ankle hard against the door. I shriek in pain as another hand snakes through the opening and grips around my knee. Matt's shoulder appears in between the door and frame and begins to widen the opening.

As he yanks, I lose my footing and fall to the hard, concrete ground. I claw at the floor, trying to get away as he practically bursts his way through the door. In seconds, he is looming over me and grips me around the waist, yanking me up in the air.

Carrying me over his shoulder again, this time with more effort as he's hurt and limping, we go through the doorway and down the dark stairwell, my hope of getting away dwindling with every step down.

Chapter Twenty-Six

Jack walked into the garage and scanned the dirty concrete room for any trace of Maddie. When his focus landed on a scattered pile of the flower petals in front of a door, he was both happy and scared. Until now, she'd only scattered two or three petals here and there; now it looked like she emptied her pockets before heading through this door.

Once he crossed the space, he cracked open a heavy metal door and peered inside. All he saw was darkness. Holding his breath, he strained to listen. When silence greeted him, he started to pry open the door all the way but then paused when an image of Ben's angry face flashed through his head. He quickly pulled out his phone, called him and explained the situation. Within moments, his friend ran through the open garage door, gun in hand. Upon seeing Jack, he slowed down to a walk and holstered his gun.

"Jack, I think you should—"

"Ben, shut up," he said as he yanked the door open.

Before he could step through, Ben moved in front of him. "I've got the gun. You could at least let me go first."

Jack gave a terse nod and the two of them began a slow descent down the dark stairs.

Once they glided past the first landing, they stopped, straining to listen for any sounds. When they were met with silence, Ben took out his flashlight, letting them both examine their surroundings. The stairs went down two more stories and led to a single door, this one not looking as heavy duty as the first one proved to be. They made their way down, their movements echoing off the concrete walls and slowly opened the next door.

Greeted with another dark, long hallway, this time they quickly realized they were not alone. Voices echoed from the distant end of the hallway.

"Shut up."

"Then put me down you piece of—yow!"

The sound of a smack echoed off the walls and Maddie's voice rang out. Every bit of air rushed out of Jack's lungs. Someone was hurting her. He surged forward but Ben's hand quickly shot out across his chest.

He knew his friend was trained for dangerous situations like this, and he trusted him with his life, but it took everything for Jack to just nod in agreement, letting him take the lead. In response, Ben quickened his pace, taking the lead down the hallway.

Moving at a faster pace now, they heard the group up ahead stop short.

"Someone's here," A male voice whispered.

"Help—oof."

Jack heard the distinct sound of a palm cracking against bare skin. The sounds of running feet erupted down the hallway. Seeing red, he broke into a run, Ben at his side. The faint light at the end of the tunnel now brightened until he saw it open to the lakeside. Ben and Jack sprinted to the end, slowing up only when they reached the lip of the tunnel.

Ben cautiously peered out, looking right then left, then suddenly broke into a run with his weapon drawn, Jack followed closely.

The tunnel led them out onto the concrete walkway of the lakeshore path, leading toward the park across the street from the apartment building. Once Jack's vision adjusted to the brightness, he saw the reason Ben took off. The three men and Maddie, who was being carried over Matt's shoulder, were heading toward a Chicago Park District golf cart. It made sense as a getaway car for this area, a real car would've brought too much attention. They must be driving to another car to get out of here.

Maddie, amidst the jostling of being carried, looked up. A brief look of relief passed over her features then turned into that of concentration. Grasping her hands together, she raised them as high then brought them down hard on Matt's back. He momentarily faltered, giving her the opportunity to kick repeatedly, making contact with any body part. Her heel connected with Matt's forehead, sending him flat on his back. And Maddie flew through the air.

The two of them fell onto the grass. Matt was fast though, his hand shooting out, reaching her ankle and taking it in a grip so strong, Jack saw Maddie's wince. They were closing in when Ben yelled, "Police! Freeze!"

All four of them paused and looked back at us, surprised, and then snapped back to action. The two cronies continued for the cart, and he called out to Ben, "You get them, I've got Matt."

The aches and pains from his injuries melted away as pure adrenaline kicked in and Jack sped up, coming upon Matt and Maddie. Seeing him, Matt let go of Maddie and jumped up. He was seething with rage and began to stalk toward Jack. He slowed down as he got within a foot of him and it hit him just how much taller Matt was than him. He must have been doing steroids or some sort of drug because he was big but not big enough to warrant this crazy superhuman strength.

Jack swung the bat at Matt. He caught the bat in his hand and started trying to pull it out of his grip. The knight in shining armor plan for Maddie was starting to crumble as Jack desperately tried to hold onto the weapon. He held on and it occurred to him that now they were just playing tug of war with this bat. Grunting, he felt the cut on his cheek start to open again as the blood pumped hard throughout his body. He risked a glance at Maddie, who was slowly getting to her feet, her palm pressed against her cheek.

Using that moment of distraction to his advantage, Matt's fist suddenly connected with the left side of his face, and put him to the ground. Jack looked up as his attacker came closer, breathing heavy, face beet-red. Staring at him, eyes crazy, he tossed the bat down, then kicked Jack in the chest. "You think you can beat me?"

Another kick landed. Through the blinding pain, Jack's breathing became ragged, and he tried to hold onto Matt's foot. "Do you think—aahhh."

Matt stumbled forward, back arching. Jack looked around and saw Maddie with the bat in both hands. She was breathing hard as she advanced forward. Matt turned but before he could do anything, she lifted the bat again and swung with such force it smacked him across his face and splinters flew. His eyes rolled into the back of his head. Matt's knees buckled and Jack managed to scramble out of the way as he crashed down in a perfect faceplant. A sickening thud sounded out as he made contact with the grass. He lay there, unmoving.

Maddie stared at his unmoving body, breathing hard. Dropping the piece still in her hand she walked toward her ex-boyfriend and prodded his shoulder with a noticeably swollen foot. She glanced down at the bat that now lay in pieces on the grass, then looked up at Jack. "Sorry I broke your bat."

"Maddie."

Struggling to get to his feet, the movement managed to snap her out of the shock. Immediately she was at his side, helping him stand as straight as possible. Her eyes watered as she swept her fingertips over his face and upper body.

"I'm so sorry, Jack. I…are you okay?"

He nodded and looked over to where the other two goons stood. Ben had them both on the ground, one in handcuffs, the other restrained by Ben's body weight. He was talking into the walkie talkie clipped to his shirt collar.

Jack knew it was over. Everything was over. As his breath began to even out, he looked over at Maddie.

Her brown wavy hair was a mess, tangled and sticking up. Her mascara was smeared on one side of her face and although she looked tired, her wide eyes were alert. There was a bruise forming over her cheek, but no other visible wounds appeared besides her swollen ankle and favoring her left side. Her breathing was beginning to get back to normal but still sounded a bit labored and her hand, still in his, squeezed tight but shook slightly.

With the late summer sun beaming down on her disheveled state, she was still one of the most beautiful women Jack had ever beheld. He loved her. Turning, he moved his free hand to her face and gently cupped her cheek, getting her to look him in the eyes. "We're okay."

"We're okay," she repeated, pressing her warm cheek against his palm. He pulled her head toward him and rested her head on his shoulder while he looked around.

The sounds of sirens grew louder as Jack saw police cars pulling up to the park area. He shouldn't be surprised that they arrived there so quickly, they did only end up across the street. After the influx of officers relieved Ben, he got up and walked over to the couple.

"Maddie, I'm glad to see—ooofff—"

One moment she was standing next to him, looking exhausted. The next, she let go of Jack's hand to launch herself at Ben, wrapping both arms around his neck. "Thank you."

Ben looked so startled Jack barely stifled a laugh. He looked at him a little bewildered. At his nod of encouragement, Ben brought his hands up and returned the embrace.

After a moment she relinquished her hold and straightened up, shaking her head and holding her chin up high. "I know you're not my biggest fan but I feel I've earned the right to say I told you I didn't do it. I knocked Matt out because he was hurting Jack. In total there were three bags filled with valuables. They made me use my card to take them up to the penthouse because they threatened Jack, I swear I had nothing to do with it. I—"

"Okay, okay." Ben held his hands in front of him, motioning for her to slow down. "I'm not going to take your statement right now but thanks for saving Jack's ass. I'm glad he's got you now." He turned his attention to his friend. "Go to the medics and get checked out right now." With that, he walked past us toward the waiting horde of cops.

Maddie's eyes snapped back to Jack, full of concern. "Oh my gosh why are you still standing? Let's go."

"I'm only going if you get checked out first" Jack said, making it a point to look down at her ankle.

She waved off his demand and wrapped her arm under his armpits and across his back, giving him support as they started their walk to the ambulance that arrived. He let her do this, all the while making sure not to put too much weight on her as she was now definitely limping.

"I should get hurt more often if it means having your hands on me like this—ow!" She pinched his arm. "Hey, I'm hurt here, you can't pinch me."

"You'll live."

"You know how I feel about your hands. Your beautiful, elegant, magical hands…"

She smiled and shook her head. He suddenly stopped walking and she became concerned again. "What? Do you need them to come to you? Can you not walk anymore? Are you in pain?"

"No, I just realized my hands aren't tied anymore so I can do this."

He slid his hands into her hair and brought her lips up to his. He didn't care that they were standing in the middle of a crime scene with cops walking past them and people staring at them from behind tape. He kissed her, trying to place all his feelings into the act. He felt the tension in her body melt and her hands rested atop his arms. He stopped only when he felt the absolute need to breathe again and broke the kiss but kept his face close to hers. Her eyes were still closed but her lips had turned up into a small smile.

"I love you."

Her eyes snapped open in shock, but her mouth stayed in that smile. Before she got a chance to say anything, he kept talking.

"I've only known you a short time and I know we just went through a crazy…thing but it's giving me adrenaline to say what I've been feeling for a while now. I love you. I'm crazy about you. I think you're one of the most kind, beautiful, brave people I've ever met and I love you and I can't stop saying it. I love you."

She began to cry, and he swiped his thumb over her cheek, brushing away the tears. "You don't have to say anything. I just needed you to know."

"I love you, too. I know I said it in the heat of the moment up there but I meant it." Even though her voice came out cracked and full of emotion, he thought it was the most wonderful thing he had ever heard.

"I came and accidentally assisted a robbery because I love you so much so you're obviously dumb if you think I didn't mean it."

He laughed and winced as his ribs jolted with pain. "You also saved my ass from being beaten. Have I told you how sexy you were? Swinging that bat?" He kissed her again and again as she laughed and finally stopped him by pulling away.

"Come on, lover boy. Let's get you checked out."

She entwined their fingers and led him to the paramedics who gave him a once over to make sure he was not about to drop dead. Even as they poked and prodded him, Maddie didn't let go of his hand and he couldn't seem to wipe the dopey smile off his face.

Chapter Twenty-Seven

One Week Later

We gave Matt and Kent some serious lumps on their heads, and concussions to go with them. Other than that, they were fine. The plan had been to take the waiting golf cart, all loaded up and go quickly to a waiting car which would've taken us all to Indiana. I shudder thinking about what that car trip would've been like. Apparently, they had a house stashed with all the loot they previously stolen.

I can't remember which goon broke first but he basically sang like a canary when brought into the interrogation room. I begged Jack to talk Ben into letting me watch, because how cool would that have been, but I wasn't allowed.

I saw Matt when I was at the hospital with Jack who thankfully only had bruised ribs and a plethora of scrapes and bruises. As someone who was manhandled, I only turned out to have a bone bruise on my ankle in addition to the one on my face, we were both lucky, I guess. Matt was handcuffed to a gurney and looking miserable. When we made eye contact, he tried to call out to me. I responded with a lovely middle finger for him to admire.

Ben joined us at the hospital, and I got to give him an official statement which honestly, was kind of thrilling. I'm pretty sure I gave him a fantastic account because he barely asked any follow up questions. This also could have been because I kept making comments like, "and that's why *they* were the bad guys and not me," which caused Ben to look ashamed of himself.

Of course, I've forgiven him, but I don't mind making him squirm for a bit more.

Jack took off work for a few days and I helped him clean his place up and per his request, nursed him back to health...which led me to spend almost every night at his house.

This, however, did not make Sarah and Stephanie very happy. On the way back from the hospital, I spent almost a half an hour placating them, telling them I was all right and that the whole ordeal was finished. I heard Sarah sniffle while Stephanie ranted about how terrible Matt was and how she would hurt him in some very creative ways. It took Jack wrestling the phone from my grip and telling the girls that he needed me to take care of him to get them off the phone.

Now it's a week later and one of my last days of summer before the new school year starts. I'm currently home, sitting on my porch, drinking wine with Jack next to me. His cuts and bruises have pretty much healed and he's back to looking perfect. I'm staring at him as he stares at his phone, smiling.

"You're staring at me."

I jump at his voice and chuckle, he looks up at me, still smiling and reaches over, grabbing my hand. He begins to pull, moving me out of my chair and onto his lap. My arm goes around his neck and my legs are draped over his, his arms are tightly secured around me.

"So, I have to tell you something."

I frown and shrug my shoulders. "Should I be worried?"

He takes a deep breath and looks away; I start to get a bad feeling in my stomach. "Now that we're officially together, I can no longer be your legal representation."

I let out the breath I didn't realize I was holding and lightly smack him on the back of the head as he laughs. He pulls me closer. "I'm sorry I couldn't resist."

"You'll be sorry when I do resist you later."

His face nears mine and our lips are mere inches apart. "I'll make it up to you."

His lips touch mine and I can't help but melt into his embrace. He pulls my relaxed frame tighter to him and drags his lips away trailing kisses across my cheek and down my neck. I revel in the feeling of his scruff against my sensitive skin and a soft moan escapes my lips. I can feel him begin to harden underneath me and I start to push against his chest.

"I have school next week and I can't show up with a hickey." I feel him smile against my throat.

"It'll be gone by then."

I laugh as I hear the door open behind us and my roommate's step outside, their hands filled with snacks and drinks. "Not that we don't love you two together but let's keep it PG out here."

"Why would you want that? We've provided you with a seat since we're sharing a chair," Jack says, his arms securely holding me in place. I can still feel how hard he is underneath me and give him a knowing look. His fingers dig into my side, tickling me, and I squirm.

"Where are all these friends of yours Maddie keeps telling us about?" Sarah teases. "They're not coming to celebrate? Are they even real?"

"They're meeting up with us later at the bar, that way when they inevitably say something embarrassing about me, it'll be easier to pass it off as a result of alcohol."

During the time I stayed over at Jack's place, I was treated to visits from all of his childhood friends. They were a rowdy bunch and brought a smile to Jack's face that made my heart practically burst. I liked them instantly and immediately bullied Jack into giving me their numbers so we could hang out as a group more.

"Yeah, I texted them, they're excited to meet you guys."

Jack looks at me and smiles, shaking his head. "Should I be worried? You texting all my friends? Looking to replace me?"

I grab his face in my hands bringing our noses to the point of touching. "You're crazy if you think I'm ever going to replace you." He leans further in giving me a kiss and playfully nipping my bottom lip.

"Enough love birds, the episode is about to play!"

The news about the gang of robbers being caught has spread far and wide. To my delight, it caught the attention of RJ and *Murder for Your Thoughts*.

Mine and Jack's names had not been mentioned in any stories, but she must've had a good inside source because she reached out to us via email for a quick interview. When I started crying out of excitement, Jack begrudgingly agreed to do it with me and it was airing, tonight.

"Hello Murder Heads! Tonight I have a quick update and interview about an ongoing drama that's been happening in Chicago before I go on to talk about the Murders at White House Farm.

"As a reminder, there have been a bunch of robberies at high end apartment buildings in the upscale

Gold Coast neighborhood of Chicago. They've been eluding police and stealing from the rich, a real Robin Hood type gang except for being total jerks rather than helping the poor.

"My reach is far and wide which has led me to having many sources and friends in law enforcement. Some of those friends led me to Maddie Conor, a twenty-nine-year-old teacher from Chicago and devoted Murder Head herself, who was instrumental in the downfall of this almost unstoppable gang. I spoke with her along Jack Delgado, her lawyer boyfriend who also stopped the bad guys.

RJ: *So you guys, how did you get involved?*

Maddie: *Well I actually had begun to suspect Matt—*

Jack: *Her ex*

Maddie: *Yes, my ex. He was acting odd and had begun to hint to me that he was doing something illegal. Meanwhile, I didn't realize it but he had actually taken one of my bracelets and planted it in one of the apartments they had broken into, framing me.*

Jack: *Yeah so while the police had no leads on the actual robbers, they suspected Maddie which was insane. So then they basically kidnapped her and—*

Maddie: *Um actually they threatened Jack and held him hostage—*

Jack: *Okay I got out later—*

Maddie: *Yeah, because you snuck up on a guy*

My roommates look over at us with amused looks. I rub Jack's back in a comforting and apologetic way as he shakes his head in exasperation, mumbling, "You couldn't have just let me sound cool…"

I give him a kiss on the temple and murmur in his ear, "I'll make it up to you later." Which earns me a searing look, making me feel warm all the way down to my toes.

"Shhhh—" Steph interrupts us, "—It's still going!"

I tune back in to hear my voice.

Maddie: *—had a way out through the garage. Apparently, there was a route that led to the lake front and they would've gone from there.*

RJ: *And so what was the actual plan?*

Maddie: *Well...um I-I actually re-read one of your blog posts...*

RJ: *Oh really?*

Maddie: *Yeah it was about the history of the listening device and it gave me the idea to try and get these guys to admit something on tape. I called Ben—*

Jack: *One of my best friends and also one of Chicago's finest*

Maddie:—*who was not happy that I was going but I kept him on the phone while I spoke to the guys...*

Jack: *Until they found your phone and smashed it.*

Maddie: *Yeah, but I'm sure Ben heard and like, recorded some good stuff—*

Jack: *Which we won't be able to discuss until legal proceedings are complete*

Maddie: *Oops, yeah he's right.*

RJ: *Well it was so great to meet you guys and I'm so flattered that you're a fan because now I'm a fan of you.*

I cringe internally as I remember starting to tear up from the excitement of RJ saying this to me and I feel Jack's arms tighten around my waist.

"You guys, that was so great," Sarah exclaims, raising a glass in our direction and silently cheering us.

Steph nods as she begins to stand. "I also loved it and I'll get us more wine to celebrate properly."

Sarah takes one look at us and says, "Let me help you with that."

As my friends leave Jack and me alone, I look down at him and smile. He adjusts himself so that his face is closer to mine. "You know, I'm glad I let you talk me into doing that interview."

"You are?"

"Because I've already planned on how you're going to make it up to me. It involves a very in-depth tour of my apartment."

I pout at this. "I can't make it up to you tonight in my own room?"

His eyes flare with heat and he grins, sending another jolt of excitement through me. "Oh this is a twofold process. So we'll start here tonight, pack some things, and then continue at mine tomorrow."

I pull back slightly, confusion all over my face but he continues. "Part of the tour will concern showing you your side of the closet and nightstand which I cleared out for you."

I'm stunned and sit there with my eyes wide and my mouth in an *O*. His grin begins to twitch, and I can see uncertainty creeping into his face. He starts talking again. "That is, if you want to keep some things at my house. I just figured that with school starting up, you'll have to get up earlier and I didn't want anything stopping you from spending the night at my house and—"

I stop him from talking by pressing my lips to his and I feel his shoulders drop the tension that crept into them. His arms tighten even more around me as my hands cup his face and I continue to kiss him. Only when I need to take a breath do I pull away but not before I give a small nibble to his bottom lip.

He's slightly dazed with a dopey grin on his face. "I take it you're into that idea?"

I smile as the back of my knuckles stroke his scruffy cheek. "I am actually a big fan of that idea because I had the same one. You've got a drawer here, too."

Jack throws his head back with a loud laugh and stands up with me still in his arms, a move that has me gripping onto him for dear life, seeing as we're on a second-floor balcony. Taking notice of my now death-like grip, he grins even harder.

"You're crazy if you think I'm going to drop you. Maddie, I'm never letting you go."

As he walks us back inside, toward my room, I can't help but think for the first time ever how excited I am for the summer to be over and to start the next chapter.

Epilogue

Ben

I bring the glass of whisky to my lips and take a small sip as I sit in my apartment staring at the TV but not really watching it. This is my ritual after a long shift. When I put in extra time to try and fast track my career and all I do is stare at a computer screen for hours, trying to study for the detectives exam, all I can do is come home, make myself a drink and think.

My phone buzzes and I see a notification of a text for my friends. Jack has texted a picture of the inside of his closet now with both his items and Maddie's. He follows up the image with a text.

—*Look my closet looks like a grown up closet now. No more blank space!* —

The boys start responding, making jokes at Jack's expense saying he's whipped now but I just smile and put my phone down. I admit I'm a little jealous. I've known Jack for a long time now and I've never seen him as happy as when he's with Maddie. It's like he's finally complete.

I sigh and look out my window as I lean back in the soft leather chair that was a hand-me-down from my uncle. I hear the distant sound of a siren and the laughter of girls on the street below.

Once I make detective, once I don't have to devote

full days and work terrible shifts, that's when I'll start trying to date again.

I jump as I hear the ping of my phone go off again and look down to see Jack sending another photo, this time of Maddie putting toiletries in his bathroom. Sighing once again, I go and search "dating apps" downloading the first one that pops up. Maybe it wouldn't hurt to start looking sooner rather than later…

A word about the author…

Emilie Barage is a Chicago native who loves true crime and romance. She received her master's in Classics and works in marketing during the day and by night writes romance novels and is the co-host of the romance podcast Femmes Reading Filth.

When she's not busy doing a million projects, you can find her drinking coffee, doing improv or just being with the people she loves!